Gymnast Gilly
The Champ

PETER AYKROYD

Gymnast Gilly
The Champ

Illustrated by Annette Olney

ARMADA

Gymnast Gilly the Champ was first published
in the UK in Armada in 1988

Armada is an imprint of the Children's Division,
part of the Collins Publishing Group,
8 Grafton Street, London W1X 3LA

Printed in Great Britain by
William Collins Sons & Co. Ltd, Glasgow

Chapter 1

Gilly Denham was scared. She could feel her heart beating and her stomach seemed to have a lead weight in it. In a few minutes, she was going to be presented to thousands of people in the spotlights of Wembley Arena before the most important competition of her life. She had performed in front of crowds at other gymnastic events, so why was she feeling so nervous?

Pull yourself together, Gilly, she told herself sharply. You can't let your friends and yourself down after all the hard work you've done this year . . .

Gilly was standing in a narrow passage under the main stand at Wembley with the 15 other competitors – boys and girls – taking part in the grand finals of the Junior Champion Gymnast competition. She was wearing the bright yellow tracksuit worn by members of her club, Lynx, the Lincston Gymnastics Club. On her chest was the club's badge, the snarling head of a lynx. Below the lynx's head was a smaller badge of a rampant lion showing its claws which Gilly wore with just as much pride.

The eight boys and eight girls in the finals were competing not only for the title of Junior Champion Boy or Junior Champion Girl but also for the prize of large grants to help with their training.

'Many of the past winners have used their grants to train in other countries,' Christine Nesbitt, Gilly's coach, had told her when the idea of taking part in the competition had come up. 'And anyone doing well finds the experience does wonders for their gymnastics career. After all, it's a national championship which is seen by millions on TV.'

Gilly shivered. Since then, several months had gone by, months of long training sessions with Christine and John Hanley, the chief coach at Lynx, to learn new moves and routines just for this event. And now that she had got into the finals, she was as nervous as a complete novice tackling her first floor exercise in public. For what seemed the hundredth time, she patted her fair hair to make sure it was still tidy.

She wished that Marcia Cherry, her best friend, was with her. But Marcia was now sitting in the huge audience with nearly a hundred members, parents and friends of the Lynx club who had come up to Wembley in special coaches. To her embarrassment, several of her friends had brought a large yellow banner to wave. Its red letters proclaimed: *Gymnast Gilly – Lynx Supergirl*. Still, it was wonderful to have such terrific support among all those thousands of people.

'Not long to go.' The competition steward with them broke into her thoughts, giving her a big wink. He was wearing a blue blazer and had radio headphones over his ears to keep in contact with the control desk in the arena. Soon he would hear when he could let the gymnasts run out, pair by pair, waving to the crowds, on to the podium – the huge brightly-lit stage where they were to be presented and where they would perform.

Ahead of her in the passage, she could see the tall figure of Mary Weston, the one gymnast whom Christine had warned her about. Mary was already a schools international for her age group and a brilliant career in the sport had been forecast for her.

'She's a fantastic vaulter and one of the best junior floor performers in the country,' Christine had explained after Mary had won the north zone Junior Champion Gymnast finals. 'But I reckon you could surprise her on bars and beam. You're not too bad yourself.'

It was great of Christine to have said that, thought Gilly as she looked at the blue tracksuited figure of her rival from Yorkshire. But then her coach had always expected her to come up with the impossible.

Nine months ago, Gilly had never heard of Mary Weston. Indeed, nine months ago, she had never considered that she had a chance of doing well in the Junior Champion Gymnast competition, although she wasn't doing too badly in gymnastics.

Her successes outside the club had begun last year

when she was picked to train with the county squad. Then she had won the county championship for her age group, going on to become her age group regional champion and a member of the regional squad.

'You're one of the best gymnasts in the club,' Marcia had said only the other day. 'We'll see your name in bright lights yet.'

Life for Gilly had changed a great deal in the last year. It was now centred mostly on the Lynx club headquarters which was based in the former old factory down by the canal. Nearly everyone connected with the club – girls, boys, parents, coaches – had helped to convert the building into what all Lynx members believed to be one of the best gyms in the region.

John Hanley had said that he thought the club had all the equipment and facilities to produce outstanding gymnasts and even a top champion before long. To prove his point, within the year the Lynx senior girls' team had come in the top ten at the British team championships.

However, Gilly knew that excellent facilities alone were not enough to shape champions. Would-be stars had to have expert knowledge of the sport and that could only come from well-trained coaches. She and the other promising gymnasts at Lynx were certainly lucky to have John and Christine to instruct them. Both of them were always going away on courses to learn about new developments in the sport.

The other vital aspect of becoming a top gymnast was that of time. And time was something Gilly never seemed to have enough of. She was now training four or five evenings at the club and she hardly had a moment to enjoy other things. Outside the club, she saw very little of school or family friends. Very often, her weekends were taken up with competitions which usually involved travel to gyms or sports centres some distance away. Many times she had to say 'no' to invitations to go to parties or discos. If it wasn't for Marcia, Gilly knew that she could easily feel lonely.

Frequently after evening training she felt exhausted or was bruised from falls. Now and then, her hands felt like they were on fire after a long session of swinging on the asymmetric bars. At other times, she came close to tears when nothing went right for her – such as learning a new move. It was when she felt really low that she sometimes asked herself: is gymnastics worth all the hard, tiring effort it takes?

Her parents were concerned at times, too – Mrs Denham worried that Gilly was wearing herself out, and her father worried that her schoolwork was suffering. Mr Denham was in a way more closely involved with his daughter's gymnastics career than his wife.

In the first place, he spent a great deal of his time driving Gilly in the family car to the club or to competitions, and secondly, he had to find most of the money to pay Gilly's expenses such as subscriptions to the club and entry fees to championships. On top of that, Richard, Gilly's brother, was a member of the boys' section of the club and he was also showing signs of becoming a skilful gymnast.

'The two of you,' said Mr Denham one day at breakfast, 'are costing me a lot of time and money. I don't mind that but I would if I knew you weren't enjoying it. And how you do your homework properly every night, Gilly, I just can't imagine.'

Mrs Denham agreed. 'Nothing is worth that much trouble if you're going to feel tired all the time.'

Gilly jumped to her feet. 'For heaven's sake, ever since I became a gymnast, both of you haven't stopped worrying about whether I can cope with the training. Well, I'll tell you again; I can – and what's more, I find it a lot of fun, every bit of it.' She paused, and then put her arms around her mother's neck to kiss her. 'Sorry, I didn't mean to say it like that. But I do want to become a good gymnast. And I can't do that without trying my hardest.'

Mr Denham sighed. 'Gilly, we know you'd like to do well. We'll back you all the way, but we just don't want you to overdo it.'

'Dad, don't worry. I'll tell you if I can't handle it. I promise.'

Despite the hard grind, Gilly was determined to become a top competitor. She knew that John and Christine thought that she was making good progress and she worked hard at her training to become even better. While nobody in the club mentioned it, she had a feeling that she had a good chance of becoming the junior regional champion before long.

With this goal in mind, she carried on with her training sessions, Marcia giving her every encouragement and even bits of advice such as: 'You got height on that somi but your legs were a bit adrift. You'd lose points on that one, that's for sure.'

When Gilly had first joined Lynx, Marcia had been a gymnast longer than she had and therefore had been a better performer than she was. But now Gilly had caught her up and had overtaken her. However, Marcia always trained with her and had become a great help by telling Gilly exactly how she had performed certain moves. Marcia was hoping to become a qualified coach when she had finished her career as a gymnast.

Gilly's training was usually in three parts, all of which took place under the watchful eyes of Christine and sometimes John. The first part was physical preparation in which she carried out exercises to improve her three Ss – strength, suppleness and stamina. Then she tackled skills – the learning of new moves – on the four pieces of apparatus: the vault, asymmetric bars, beam and floor.

Finally, gymnast and coach would spend the rest of the time available on exercise construction, the planning of routines on each apparatus.

How well Gilly was improving she had no idea until one evening when John telephoned her parents and asked whether they and Gilly could come around to the club as he and Christine had something 'very important' to discuss with them.

'What have you been up to?' asked Mr Denham with a surprised look at his daughter. 'Nothing naughty, I hope.'

'Of course not, Dad. I haven't an inkling what they want to talk about. It may have nothing to do with me, of course.'

Father and daughter smiled at each other, both knowing that the coaches would not ask them to the club for a chat if they did not have Gilly's gymnastics career in mind.

Later, when the Denhams were sitting in the club office with cups of coffee, John and Christine made a proposal which left Gilly dazed and struggling for words. Even her parents were speechless at first.

John did not waste time. 'Christine and I believe that Gilly is an exceptional gymnast for her age. She has shown many times that she has the courage, willpower and intelligence to become one of the best young performers in the country. We therefore think that she should have a crack at the next Junior Champion Gymnast competition.'

'Junior Champion Gymnast!' cried Gilly. 'But that's a national competition. You've got to be really good – really, really good – to go in for that!'

Christine nodded. 'We believe that you have a great

11

chance of doing well in it. Mind you, you can't just enter it and expect success from the start. You'll have to have lots of extra training for it, including learning and polishing up several new moves.'

Mr and Mrs Denham sat in silence while John explained that Gilly would first have to compete at regional level. If she was one of the best two, she would then enter a zone final for the south of the country. The four leading girls from that final would then go into the grand finals at Wembley against four north zone girls. If Gilly did well in the competition, she would be in sight of the top levels of the sport, very likely as an international performer. Incidentally, next year she would be too old to enter.

'It seems a long, hard haul to Wembley,' said Mrs Denham at last. 'Do you really think Gilly should try for it?'

'She's spending a lot of time on gymnastics as it is,' Mr Denham pointed out. 'How will she fit in the extra hours? To be honest, I'm not all that keen on Gilly taking on even more training.'

Christine glanced at Gilly. 'I've thought of that. If she's game, I can give her some extra personal coaching at the club after school.'

John nodded. 'As I said, Christine and I are confident that Gilly has the ability and guts to shine in the competition, but we need to know now whether she is going in for it. Even though the grand finals are nine months away, we have to send in an entry form and, of course, start her on her special training. That's why we need your approval.'

'What do *you* think about it, Gilly?' asked her father. 'Win or lose, this Junior Champion Gymnast caper could be very hard work.'

With her heart beating, Gilly said slowly, 'I would love

to have a bash at it. I may never have such a wonderful chance again.'

Her eyes flicked from side to side as she studied her parents' faces in turn. Please say it's okay for me to do it, she pleaded in silence. She remembered that a long time ago she was in much the same situation, waiting for her parents to decide whether she could join the Lincston Gymnastics Club.

After what seemed an age, Mrs Denham said to her husband, 'She's right. If it's a good opportunity for her, she must take it. After all, if everything gets too much for her, she can always quit.'

Gilly's eyes flashed, 'I'll never do that, Mum! Not in a million years!'

Then she relaxed with relief as her father laughed. 'There's no holding you back, is there, my girl! Right, if you think you can do it, then get on with it. She's in your hands, Christine. By the way, we expect some free tickets for the Wembley grand finals . . .'

From then on, Gilly had even less time to herself than she had before. After school, she went straight to the gym club in Manton Street. On most days, Marcia came with her and helped Christine in the gym if she was needed. Sometimes, John joined them to offer his advice. At that time of day, the gym was usually empty. After an hour or so, Gilly would go home, do her homework, have something to eat and then go back to the club. When training was finished, she went straight back home to bed.

Marcia was thrilled that her friend was aiming for the Junior Champion Gymnast title. It was she more than anyone who kept Gilly's spirits up. 'Good old Gill! That tumble run is worth a medal by itself!'

Gilly was not so confident. Christine had prepared a list of moves which she had to practise again and again under strict supervision. The list included a famous but difficult vault – the Tsukahara, named after the Japanese gymnast who invented it. Gilly was performing it in the piked version. As she wrote in her training notebook:

The piked Tsukahara needs a very fast run-up to the springboard. As you jump off the board, you must be stretched and straight, with your arms swinging fast at the top of the vaulting horse. During the first flight – when you come on to the horse – you must make a full half turn on, with all your body tight and turning as one. Then you must strike and thrust off the horse with your hands before your body reaches the vertical. As you thrust off, your body must be straight. Then you must pike fast as you begin the backward somersault, bending your legs at the hips, bringing your knees towards your face, and pulling with your hands in behind the thighs. When you see the ground, straighten out at the hips, and absorb the landing with your knees and legs.

Gilly had to learn the piked Tsukahara step by step to get her timing and balance right. She also had to improve her sprinting so that she ran up to the horse at the speed necessary to rotate off it properly.

There were other moves on Christine's list which Gilly had to perfect. They included giant swings on the asymmetric bars – complete circles of the top bar – and a double twisting back somersault on the floor. All the moves had to be repeated, repeated, repeated until Gilly got them right.

Christine also began searching for new music to use in Gilly's floor exercise. The music had to vary in speed and rhythm and suit Gilly's happy personality. Natasha Oakley, the club's dance coach and the mother of Gilly's great friend Tanya who was at dancing school, was asked to advise them on the dance moves of the exercise.

Natasha was delighted to help Gilly whom she liked. Gilly had attended dance classes in Lincston so her floor work already had some graceful dance style in its movements.

When Gilly was not carrying out her special training, she joined the Lynx elite squad as normal. Here, she was with girls who had performed with her in Lynx junior teams – girls such as Shani Patel, Vanessa Dugdale and Dierdre Nicholson.

But there were other friends, too, who gave Gilly whole-hearted support when she was performing. They were Hazel Henshaw, Melanie Wood and Stephanie Daley, all of whom with Gilly had helped to track down some vandals – tough men who had tried to drive the club away from Manton Street by damaging the building when it was being converted.

These girls turned up to cheer Gilly on at the regional final of the Junior Champion Gymnast competition at Merlinford Sports Centre. While they were delighted that Gilly came second, Christine and Gilly herself were deeply disappointed with her performance, even though she qualified for the south zone final in a few weeks time.

'You've got a long way to go if you're going to make your mark in the competition,' observed Christine. 'I know you got through, but you weren't up against very good gymnasts. Your beam exercise is still terribly shaky; you were wobbling away as if you were walking on jelly.'

However, Gilly was otherwise improving noticeably and both Christine and John had every hope that she would do well in the zone finals.

Just before the zone finals, John came up with a big surprise for the club. He called a meeting at Manton Street gym for all members, parents and coaches as he had important news which affected everyone. That evening the gym was full, with people sitting everywhere –

on mats, benches and chairs. The Denhams sat with the Cherrys and Gilly naturally beside Marcia.

John's announcement was thrilling indeed. He told his audience that because the Lynx senior girls' team had done so well in the national championships, the club with others had been invited to send a dance group with the British contingent to the *gymnaestrada* at Heldenstadt in Austria that spring.

'What's a *gymnaestrada*?' asked Marcia in a loud whisper.

Gilly shook her head. 'Don't know,' she replied.

'Quiet!' said Mr Cherry. 'It's a kind of gymnastics festival. Just listen.'

John explained that if the club accepted the invitation, the group would consist of about 48 girls and their coaches. They would be under the instruction of Natasha Oakley and would fly out to Austria for a week in holiday time with the other British teams. Some senior Lynx boys had been asked to join a display being presented at the *gymnaestrada* by the Woodfield Eagles, a well-known boys' club in the region. Everyone going would have to find their own air fare.

He concluded, 'It's a great honour for Lynx to be asked. It could be an expensive honour, though. That's why we need to make a decision straightaway so that we can think about raising money and putting on a worthwhile display. Now could we have some views?'

By the end of the evening, Lincston Gymnastics Club had decided enthusiastically to accept the invitation to the Heldenstadt *gymnaestrada*. A committee was set up to organize the trip and to raise funds towards the club's expenses. At the weekend, auditions were going to be held to pick the girls for the display team.

Gilly sat glumly as excited voices sounded all around her. That counts me out, she thought. I've got to do the

Junior Champion Gymnast lark whether I like it or not. She couldn't help feeling a little sad as Marcia, bubbling away, was obviously looking forward to going to Austria and having lots of fun. It also seemed that most of her other friends were keen to go, too.

Christine went up to John after the meeting. 'There's no way that Gilly Denham is going to Austria. Nor me for that matter.'

John agreed immediately. Gilly would need every spare moment to train with Christine for the Junior Gymnast competition. She had too much at stake to be distracted by taking part in the *gymnaestrada* dance project.

And so Gilly resigned herself to more weeks of long, hard training by herself while her friends practised happily for their big adventure abroad . . .

Once again, the voice of the Wembley competition steward interrupted her reverie. 'Come on, lass, you can't wait here all day. Get going!' He gave her a friendly shove.

Gilly gave him a quick half-smile, then ran down the passage, out into the glaring lights of Wembley Arena.

Chapter 2

Marcia looked up from her score sheet in horror and glanced out across the Kenborough Sports Hall where the south zone final of the Junior Champion Gymnast competition was taking place.

After her terrible bars exercise, Gilly was now in fifth position by .1 of a point and in danger of not qualifying for the Wembley grand finals. Marcia could see Gilly's worried face on the other side of the vaulting horse. Christine was obviously giving her a pep talk, as everything now depended on the floor exercise.

Gilly was definitely performing without her usual sparkle. However, her performance on the vault and beam had been reasonable enough. And none of the 13 other competing girls was that much better than her. She had landed her piked Tsukahara vault fairly steadily and her beam routine scored a 8.70 which kept her in third place.

But that bars exercise!

Marcia, and the group of Lynx girls with her, watched intently as Gilly successfully executed her straddle mount over the low bar on to the apparatus. Her routine followed its usual course; catch the high bar, swing up to front support on the high bar, circle up to handstand . . . A gasp rippled around the crowded hall as Gilly fell off heavily. Oh no! thought Marcia, that's a half-point penalty for starters.

Gilly remounted and carried on as best she could but her concentration was gone. Her handstand on the top bar was far from straight, the flow of the exercise was disrupted, and her friends were more than relieved when she reached her front somersault dismount. But the 8.35 score made them realize that she was in a desperate situation.

Gilly herself was in no doubt after Christine's tense words that she had to produce something sensational in her floor exercise to save the day. On the mat, when the head judge had acknowledged her wave, she took a deep breath and tried to sink her total attention into her routine.

Afterwards Marcia said shaking her head, 'Whew! That was really a close shave, Gills. But I reckon your tumbling

19

got you through. You certainly came up with a fantastic full twisting back somi.'

'I thought I was dreadful,' said Gilly miserably, remembering how she had taken fourth place by just .05 of a point. 'I was feeling so exhausted. I know I've squeezed into Wembley, but only just! And Christine must be really annoyed, after all her hopes for me.'

Christine was more sad than cross. She was now convinced that Gilly had no chance of a medal at Wembley. She did not say so to Gilly, but she told John what she thought. 'Can we do anything?' she asked. 'She is really off colour. Heavens, those grand finals are just weeks away!'

John thought for a few moments. 'Let her cut down on her training time and stick mostly to body preparation for the moment. A short change from her usual training may very well help her recover her form.'

John had other problems, too. Natasha Oakley was finding it difficult to assemble enough experienced gymnasts to form the dance group going to the Heldenstadt *gymnaestrada*. But when she heard that Gilly Denham was easing off her training, she, too, came straight to the club to see John. Someone like Gilly could make all the difference to the team.

'Look, if Gilly is relaxing a bit from her work load, why can't she come to Heldenstadt as a dancer? After all, it won't be for long.'

'Why? Because she has to . . .' John broke off. He suddenly realized that a whole week away from training could encourage Gilly to get back her old gusto for competition. 'You've got a brainwave there. Pop over and chat to the Denhams as soon as you can. I'll give them a ring in the meantime.'

Natasha's suggestion took Gilly by surprise. But the more she thought about going to Austria, the more she liked the sound of it. After all, she had been training solidly for a long time without a break. Her parents, too, were in favour of the trip, seeing it as a welcome change from her usual busy and strenuous life.

'It's up to you, Gilly,' said Natasha. 'But we would love to have you with us. I know you would like being a dancer.'

Gilly looked at her parents. Then her face lit up. 'I'll come – if I can raise the fare.'

Everyone laughed. 'Don't worry about that,' said Mr Denham, 'we'll all rally round to find the money. However, you better have a word with Christine about doing some kind of training for Wembley when you're away at the *gymnaestrada*.'

The result was that Christine decided that she had better come to Heldenstadt too, in case there was an opportunity for Gilly to do a bit of training for the grand finals. In the meantime, she agreed to Gilly practising with the dance group before they left for Austria.

Marcia and many of Gilly's friends were thrilled that Gilly was joining them for the *gymnaestrada*. In fact, some friends who had decided not to try for the dance group now changed their minds when they heard that Gilly was going and asked whether they could be in the team, too.

Only one girl in the club turned up her nose when she heard that Gilly was going to be in the dance team. She was Caroline Mayhew who had been bad-tempered and jealous of Gilly ever since she joined Lynx.

'I'm very grateful to you, Gilly,' said Natasha at the first rehearsal that Gilly went to. 'I now have all the dancers I need because of you.'

Gilly was startled to find that Natasha placed her in the front row of the group. Six rows with eight girls in each row made up the basic formation. But she was delighted that Marcia was positioned beside her.

Marcia's face cracked into a wide grin, 'Welcome aboard. Now you'll know what training *really* means!'

The routine which Natasha had devised was based on the warming-up exercises which all gymnasts at the club carried out before they started training or competing. The exercises were designed not only to raise body temperature but also to stretch and relax muscles.

The routine started slowly with simple but graceful arm movements but speeded up as the girls began to exercise their other muscles by bending and stretching. Then they began to move as dancers, the rows breaking up into squares and circles, allowing space for cartwheels, back flips and somersaults. The music and movements became faster and faster until everything stopped suddenly with the girls in two tight circles, one within the other, with their arms outstretched.

Gilly did not take long to grasp what she had to do and by the end of the evening she was making very few mistakes. She was also one of the chief tumblers in the display.

'Good!' cried Natasha. 'You're shaping up very well, young ladies!'

Afterwards, at the Moo-Moo Milk Bar where they often went for a milkshake, Gilly told Marcia that she hadn't had so much fun for ages. 'I wouldn't have missed this for anything,' she said with shining eyes.

'Listen,' laughed Marcia, 'you're only in the group by luck. Anyway, what may seem a first-rate routine in Lincston may seem pretty ordinary at a *gymnaestrada* in Europe, fun though it may be.'

'What do you mean? All I know about *gymnaestradas* is that they are festivals of gymnastics.' Gilly took a long, deep suck at her chocolate milkshake. 'Tell me about them. I've got some catching up to do.'

'Well, you're right. They are huge gatherings of gymnasts of all ages from countries all over the world. Thing is, these gymnasts – four-year-olds to over-70s – meet just to put on demonstrations and displays, not competitions. So you get thousands of people performing in general gymnastics, rhythmic gymnastics and acrobatic gymnastics.'

'How many gymnasts are going to Austria?' asked Gilly.

'John said 15,000 from 25 countries.'

'What – 15,000! Wow!'

'That's why our little offering could be very small pickings. By the way, at the end of the *gymnaestrada*, all the best displays take part in a big finale. Somehow, I don't think Lincston Gymnastics Club will be there.'

Gilly snorted. 'You never know. I think our routine is great, and I bet many people in Austria will like it, too.' She took another noisy suck. 'When did *gymnaestradas* start, by the way?'

'Sometime around 1953. A Dutchman called Johan Sommer organized the first big international one in Holland.'

Gilly also learned from her friend that Lynx were in a 200-strong British delegation consisting of three girls' clubs, one boys' club, 25 rhythmic gymnasts and a group of sports acrobats.

Sean O'Connor, one of the Lynx boys going with Woodfield Eagles, the boys' club, was going to write reports on the *gymnaestrada* for the *Lincston Advertiser*, the local paper. Sean's father ran the Narrow Boat pub, at the end of Manton Street near the club building.

The more Gilly heard about the *gymnaestrada*, the more excited she got about going to Heldenstadt. But

23

apart from training in the dance group, there was a great deal to be done before she went off with the club.

Everyone connected with Lynx – members, parents, coaches, friends – helped to raise funds towards the cost of going to the *gymnaestrada*. Most people took part in a large sponsored walk and came to a special and enjoyable barn dance which earned a sizeable sum of money. Others set up profitable sweepstakes and raffles, and Mr Cherry published a booklet about the trip in which local firms bought advertisements.

The *Lincston Advertiser* helped to give publicity to other events such as jumble and bring-and-buy sales organized by the mothers, the Lincston Male Voice Choir which gave a special concert in aid of the club, and Mr Dugdale, Vanessa's father, who was sponsored to play a piano for 24 hours.

Gilly herself got friends and relations to sponsor her tumbling so that she could contribute towards her air fare to Heldenstadt. That afternoon, she performed dozens of back flips in her school gym. Both her grannies and her parents turned out trumps and between them all, there was enough money for her fare and for pocket money.

So successful was the Lynx fund-raising that several girls whose parents could not afford to pay all the air fare were helped by the club's organizing committee.

In no time at all, the day arrived when the 60 people in the Lynx party found themselves in a plane flying on a Monday from London to Heldenstadt. It was Gilly's first flight but she soon lost her first feeling of fear and enjoyed every moment. Through the windows, she and Marcia could see the snow-covered Alps, the highest mountains they had ever seen. In contrast, Heldenstadt was in the southern part of Austria and when they left the plane at the airport, the weather was quite warm.

At the terminal building, outside the bustling arrivals

hall, the club stood with their suitcases and bags, wondering what was going to happen next. Gilly noticed that all the signs and advertisements were in German and she wished that she could understand at least a few words. Overlooking the airport were some of the mountains they must have flown over. Gilly could see large forests growing right up to the snow line.

Then a middle-aged couple in red blazers approached their group. With them were two girls of Gilly's age, wearing light green tracksuits. The man was tall with piercing blue eyes and the woman slim with short hair. John went up to them and shook hands.

'Hello! Lynx of Great Britain?' said the man. 'Welcome to Austria and welcome to Heldenstadt. I am Fritz Rainer and this is Gretel Hoffmann. We are from the *Gymnaestrada* Organization and we will take you by bus to the school where you are staying. We wish you a very pleasant time at the *gymnaestrada*.'

John thanked the couple for their welcome and introduced them to Christine, Natasha and the other senior coaches. Then everyone picked up their luggage and followed the Austrians to a large coach parked outside the building. On the coach, Gilly decided to sit with one of the tracksuited girls. She chose the one with a snub nose and twinkling eyes.

Gilly held out her hand, 'Hi! I'm Gilly Denham.' She hoped the girl could speak English.

The girl could indeed – almost perfectly. She shook hands and responded with a smile. 'How do you do. I am Trudi Kessler and my friend is Maria Löwenherz. We are gymnasts, too, as you can see. All of you are staying at the academy where our club is. And Maria and I will look after you when we are not performing in the *gymnaestrada* ourselves.'

Gilly looked at the badge on Trudi's tracksuit. It was a white, heart-shaped badge on which was a red lion placed sideways and showing its claws.

Trudi fingered the badge. 'This gives our club its name. It's, how you say it, the heart-of-a-lion.'

'Lionheart!' exclaimed Gilly. 'Hey, there was a king of England in the olden days – he was called Richard the Lionheart because he was so brave. Wasn't he a prisoner in this part of the world?'

'You are right,' said Trudi. 'But he was kept in a castle far away in the north of Austria. Our Lionheart name is an important part of the history of Heldenstadt here in the south.'

As the coach sped along, Trudi explained that Heldenstadt was surrounded by high mountains and blue-green lakes. In ancient times, many important roads and trade routes had met here. The tribes in the area had become fiercely independent and from the earliest times had struggled against invaders such as the Romans and Avars from the east. They fought so many battles that they became known as Lionhearts.

Heldenstadt had become the centre of the resistance to invasions and even today, as part of modern Austria, people of the region liked to imagine that they were not under the complete control of other rulers.

'We are very close to Italy,' said Trudi, 'and, of course Yugoslavia. But the nearest country is Bucania.'

'Bucania?' Gilly raised her eyebrows. 'I've never heard of it.'

'Our oldest enemies in history are the Bucanians. You know, for centuries, they tried to conquer our land. Today, Bucania is a small country, friends with the Soviet Union and its allies to the east of Europe.' Trudi sniffed in scorn. 'Okay, the Bucanians have good gymnasts, but we in Heldenstadt still do not meet with their people very

26

much – even though Grodnik, the chief city, is only three hours away by car. But that is enough history for today. Now, Gilly, you tell me about your country, about your gymnastics.'

Gilly did not quite understand about Bucania but she did not ask further questions. Instead, she told her new friend about Lincston and the Lynx gymnastics club. She showed her the club badge, which, like Trudi's, was a fierce animal.

'Tell you something,' said Gilly, 'the lion and the lynx come from the same family, don't they – the cat family.'

Trudi laughed delightedly. 'Then you and me belong to the same family!' She turned and shook hands again with Gilly.

The coach's horn sounded loudly. The girls looked out to see that they had reached the outskirts of the city.

'Not far now,' said Trudi. 'I know you will have a good time in Heldenstadt with all the gymnasts there.' With a chuckle, she added: 'You may meet some heroes, too, because in German Heldenstadt means "the town of the heroes".'

Here's hoping, thought Gilly. I'd love to meet a real live hero, someone smashing to make *me* lionhearted for when I go to Wembley . . .

Chapter 3

The St Margarethen Academy where the Lincston Gymnastics Club were staying during their week at the *gymnaestrada* was in the ancient part of Heldenstadt.

As the coach drove through the narrow streets, Gilly could see that many of the lanes and alleys were for walkers only. She caught glimpses of courtyards and fountains, of old buildings with balconies and highpointed roofs. High above the city towered the cathedral church of St Michael and through the neighbourhood stretched a thin canal made colourful by market stalls and banks of flowers. Everywhere, crowds bustled happily along in the evening sun, many people stopping by the numerous shops and coffee houses.

The Academy was formerly a convent before it became a well-known school for girls. The building itself was not only old but also very large with its own cloistered courtyard. It was empty for the week of the *gymnaestrada* because the Austrian pupils, too, were on holiday.

'Gosh!' said Marcia, looking up at the tall, round arch of the gateway entrance as she got off the coach. 'It's like some kind of old palace.'

'It's certainly different from Lincston High,' said Gilly, thinking of their time-worn grey-brick school back in Britain. As she struggled amongst a throng of Lynx girls to find her kitbag in a pile of luggage, she bumped into Trudi. 'I'm sorry,' she said with a flustered smile.

'Don't worry,' said Trudi cheerfully. 'Gilly, this is Maria Löwenherz who will help to guide your club during the *gymnaestrada*. She and I belong to this Academy both as pupils and as gymnasts.'

'Hello!' said Maria. She was fair-haired like Gilly, with high cheekbones, and held herself erect so that she seemed very tall. 'Wilkommen! Welcome to our city! I hear that you are a famous gymnast.'

'Hardly!' Gilly blushed. 'I've just been lucky enough to be in a big competition.' She looked around quickly for Marcia and beckoned her over. 'Marcia, meet Trudi Kessler and Maria Löwenherz. They're going to make sure that no Lynx girl gets lost while the *gymnaestrada* is on.'

Everyone laughed as Marcia greeted the two Austrians. Gilly went on: 'And I hope they're going to show us lots of interesting things while we're here.'

Trudi beamed. 'We promise! We will show you lovely things in Heldenstadt you will always remember. Now come with us and see where you will sleep. Then you will have your supper.'

Before long, Gilly and Marcia, with several other Lynx members, were installed in a big room with high rafters. Their hosts had provided each girl with a comfortable bed. As there were several thousand gymnasts now in the city who needed somewhere to stay, the Lynx girls knew that they were lucky to be in such a pleasant building.

The view from their windows was magnificent. Gilly looked out over red rooftops to the spire of St Michael's cathedral. Beyond it, on the other side of the city, she could see a hill with what looked like a castle on top of it.

Downstairs, the girls joined the rest of the club at supper in a huge hall with massive stained glass windows. 'It's like eating in church,' said Marcia as she munched her sardine salad. There was also a Swedish club based at the Academy, and their members, too, stared wide-eyed around the hall. Most of the Swedish girls seemed to have long blonde hair.

Christine came across to talk with Gilly, hurrying with excitement. 'Gilly, there's a fully-equipped gym here. I want you to do at least half an hour of suppling exercises before you go to bed. We can't have you going stiff just because you're in Austria.'

At first Gilly grimaced. But then she realized that Christine was right about keeping her muscles supple. So she promised to come to the gym later, in T-shirt and shorts, to do some exercises.

Maria came and sat down at their table. 'Tomorrow morning, you settle in and in the afternoon you do some practice. There are eight different halls where all the gymnasts put on their displays. You know, some of the displays have hundreds of people – like the ones from Switzerland and from here in Austria.

'Crumbs!' said Gilly. 'When does it all begin – officially?'

'On Wednesday. There is the opening ceremony in the big City Stadium. The *gymnaestrada* ends on Saturday night with the best displays going on at the Heldenhalle, our biggest arena. So your display could be chosen for the finale.'

'Only if a miracle happens,' said Marcia firmly. 'By the way, how do we get around this town of yours?'

'You will be taken by coach to your arenas. And during this week, you can ride in public buses and trams for free.'

'It all sounds very exciting,' said Gilly. 'I just hope there's time to do some sightseeing and shopping.'

Maria smiled. 'There will be time. As Trudi said, we will show you around. Ah, here is Trudi herself. What's the matter, Trudlein?'

Trudi was out of breath, with an alarmed look on her face. 'Bucania. They have been invited to the *gymnae-strada*. Fritz has just said so. Twenty-four rhythmic gymnasts. Maria, they will stay in this school!'

'So you and I have to look after them,' said Maria calmly. 'That will not be difficult.'

Trudi wrinkled her forehead in a worried frown. 'But many people will not like the Bucanians here. There could be much trouble.'

'Now how do we possibly know that? They are not even here yet. I think it is excellent and certainly time that we in Heldenstadt tried to make friends with our Bucanian neighbours. Now when do they come?'

'Tomorrow morning. We take a coach to the station to meet them.'

'*Sehr gut*! Very good! We will go then and Marcia and Gilly can come, too.' Maria glanced at the two Lynx girls. 'If you would like to.'

'I'd love to,' said Gilly excitedly.

'Me, too!' cried Marcia. 'These Bucanians sound really interesting. But you'll have to tell me why.'

By the time Gilly snuggled down in her bed with her eyes drooping with tiredness, she had explained to Marcia about the age-old hostile relationship between the peoples of Heldenstadt and Bucania. She had also carried out some gentle training with Christine in the Academy's gym which had all the usual apparatus and safety mats.

'I'm whacked!' Gilly heard Hazel Henshaw yawn just as the lights went out.

Not as much as me, she thought. Then she fell asleep.

The next morning, Gilly was woken by the unfamiliar sound of nearby church bells. For a moment she was confused. Then she realized where she was. She felt bright-eyed and alert after her deep sleep.

She leaned over and thumped Marcia in the next bed to hers. 'Wake up, lazy bones! We're going to the station, remember!'

Marcia groaned and stretched, But soon she was up and dressed, like Gilly, in her yellow Lynx tracksuit.

After a breakfast of rolls, jam and coffee, the two girls asked John whether they could go to the station with their Austrian friends to meet the Bucanian delegation. John said yes but reminded them not to forget that their dance group were practising that afternoon.

Before long, Gilly and Marcia were on their way in a large coach with Maria and Trudi. In the front of the coach sat Fritz Rainer and Gretel Hoffman, the two

32

gymnaestrada officials who had met them yesterday at the airport.

Trudi explained that Fritz Rainer had been a famous Austrian gymnast in the 1960s. 'He was in the Olympic Games and now he helps to run gymnastics in our country.' Gretel was a well-known national women's coach.

The coach was heading towards the modern part of the city which the British girls had not yet visited. But before it left the old district, it went past a large, open area which had an impressive statue in the middle of its central gardens.

'This is our main square,' said Maria.

'Look!' called Gilly. 'That statue. It's the Lionheart.'

The statue was indeed just like the badge on the tracksuits worn by the two Austrians. In front of a large, heart-shaped shield, a snarling lion stood upright, showing its claws.

Trudi nodded. 'You are right. That is the Löwenherz, the Lionheart, the crest of our city.'

'And the name of your gym club – that's Löwenherz, too?' asked Marcia.

'*Ja*,' replied Trudi. 'Yes, at the Academy we are honoured to be the Löwenherz Heldenstadt club.'

Löwenherz, thought Gilly. Where have I heard that before? Her head whirled around. 'Maria, isn't that your name as well?'

There was a pause. Then Trudi said, with a nod from Maria: 'That is correct. Her full name is Countess Maria Anastasia von Löwenherz. Her family goes back for many centuries – many centuries of our history.' She grinned. 'But we all know her as plain Maria Löwenherz.'

'A real countess – no kidding!' Marcia was stunned. 'Well, I never!'

Gilly was just as astonished, but tried not to show it.

33

But before she could stop herself, she said: 'I suppose you live in a castle.' She then felt ashamed at having made such a silly remark.

But a smile broke out on Maria's face. 'Yes, I do live in a castle – well, in a small part of one. It's called the Schloss Landskron and you may have seen it. It's on a hill not far from the cathedral.'

Gilly remembered that she had seen a castle from their room at the Academy. She mentioned this to Maria.

'That would be it,' said Maria. 'Now this evening, you, Marcia and Trudi must come and visit us. You will find the Schloss very interesting. But you will have to listen to more history!'

The girls laughed and continued to chat, mostly about gymnastics which they all loved and shared as an interest.

In a few minutes, they had drawn up at the Bahnhof, Heldenstadt's main railway station. Fritz Rainer led them to a platform entrance where they found a small crowd had gathered. A television crew was there as well and the girls could see several press photographers. A small squad of police joined them.

'See,' whispered Trudi, 'there could be trouble.'

Soon the train from Grodnik slid into the station, pulled by a big diesel locomotive. The crowd moved forward, but the police held them back, allowing just Fritz Rainer in his red blazer to go through the barrier.

From where they stood, Gilly, Marcia, Trudi and Maria could see a group of girls getting off the train who had to be the gymnasts from Bucania. They were all dressed in dark blue and red tracksuits and several carried the hoops and 19cm-wide rubber balls which were some of the hand apparatus used in rhythmic gymnastics. Most of the gymnasts gazed around them silently with timid looks on their faces.

The group was led by a woman whom Gilly thought

must have been devastatingly beautiful when she was younger. The woman had reddish hair and wide-set blue eyes, and she stood and moved with the grace of a ballet dancer.

Maria nudged Trudi, 'It's Sonia Krasna.'

'Who's she?' asked Gilly, watching the leader with interest.

'The best gymnast to come out of Bucania. People thought once she could rival Vera Caslavska.'

Both Gilly and Marcia had heard of the great Vera from Czechoslovakia. She was a world, Olympic and European champion in the 1960s and was very popular with gymnastics fans in western countries.

'Now Sonia is a respected coach at the Dynamo Club, Grodnik,' said Maria, taking in every move, every gesture made by the former star. 'Look, Fritz Rainer seems to know her very well.'

Fritz had gone up to Sonia and the couple had embraced. Sonia wiped a tear from her eye. Then Fritz led the Bucanian party through the barrier towards the coach. As they left the platform, many people in the crowd began to boo and jeer. '*Raus*! Get out, Bucanians!' someone called. 'We don't want you here.' The television and press cameramen jostled to take close-up pictures of the protesters. The police had to move in to clear a way through the throng for the gymnasts to cross the station foyer.

Gilly felt very relieved when they at last boarded the coach as she had felt a twinge of fear at the crowd. On the coach, she and Marcia helped to welcome the Bucanians and load their kit for the short journey. When the coach moved off, she found herself sitting with a small, auburn-haired gymnast who was hugging a string bag containing three white balls for rhythmic gymnastics. The gymnast, who was close to her in age, flashed a pair of dark brown eyes. 'Speak English?'

'Yes, I do. I come from Britain. I'm Gilly Denham.'

'Gilly Denham – from Britain? I learn English at school – better than Russian.' She laughed, then drew herself up proudly. 'I am Lenka Zaveska. I come to dance in the *gymnaestrada*. In Grodnik, I am just a gymnast – on the vault, bars, beam and floor.'

'Why, that's like me,' cried Gilly. But she found a big difference between their gymnastics. Lenka was good enough to have been picked out to go to a special school for sport where she was taught gymnastics as part of the work there. She was expected to become an excellent gymnast.

'You *are* lucky,' Gilly told her new friend. But she wondered if she would enjoy going to a special school for sport, if there was such a place, in her own country.

When they arrived back at the Academy, there were police outside the arched entrance. The Austrians were taking great care to prevent any more bad feeling against their Bucanian guests being shown.

Inside, the Bucanian gymnasts were given sleeping accommodation in a big room across the landing from the dormitory where Gilly and Marcia were. Then the new arrivals were taken downstairs to lunch.

Both the Swedish and British girls tried to make the Bucanians welcome but they found them very shy. Except for one.

Lenka Zaveska, still holding her string bag of balls, came and sat down with Gilly, Marcia and the two Austrian girls. She chatted away, enjoying her stew as if she had not eaten food for a week.

'We, too, have a practice this afternoon,' she said with her mouth full. 'But this evening, we will meet.'

'Yes,' agreed Maria. 'You, too, must come to the Schloss – goodness me, what is that!'

All talking stopped suddenly as two people burst into the hall who were to change not just Lenka's plans but those of the entire Bucanian delegation. They were the most frightening people Gilly had ever come across and she could never remember them afterwards without a shudder.

The two had come by car officially as Bucanian coaches but from the moment of their arrival it was clear that they were in Heldenstadt as nothing but evil-tempered minders for the gymnasts.

The man, Vaclav Zoulok, had markedly round shoulders and a large scar on his cheek which twisted his upper lip into a permanent, hideous grin. The woman was Tereza Srot, a short squat toad of a woman, with grim, pointed features.

Without any request or announcement, Zoulok and Srot took a roll call of the Bucanian team, shouting out each name. Each gymnast had to raise her hand in response.

'It's a bit much, isn't it?' muttered Marcia to no one in particular.

Then Zoulok came to the end of the list. 'Zaveska! Zaveska?'

Lenka sat still, with scorn on her face. Srot began to shuffle between the tables, looking closely at each girl. 'Zaveska? Zaveska?'

Finally, Srot croaked out in the Bucanian language what must have been a sinister threat. Then, slowly, Lenka raised her arm.

Srot pounced, and frog-marched the gymnast out of the hall, string bag of balls and all.

With the other girls, Gilly sat silent and appalled. How could they possibly enjoy their stay here if it included such horrible bullies?

Chapter 4

After lunch, the coaches of the various clubs hurried around collecting their girls together. Each club had a practice session that afternoon at one of the halls in the city and no one wanted to waste a second of precious rehearsal time.

Gretel Hoffmann, the Austrian coach, told John:

'There is a strict schedule for each hall, and if a club does not turn up at the right time, they may not be able to train for a full session.'

But soon the Swedes and the British were assembled, the Swedish girls in pastel blue tracksuits and the Lynx girls, of course, in their familiar yellow garb.

Of the Bucanians, however, there was no sign.

'I bet they've been taken away for a stern lecture, poor things,' declared Marcia as she blew some dust off her gymnastics slippers.

Gilly said nothing. She had tried to see Lenka again, but the grim shape of Tereza Srot had stopped her from approaching the little gymnast. Marcia was right; the entire Bucanian party had been driven upstairs to their sleeping quarters by their minders, no doubt for a severe reprimand.

Of Maria and Trudi, there was no sign, either. But they, like their visitors, had to practise for the *gymnaestrada* with their own club.

'We will see you later,' said Trudi, 'but now we become real Löwenherz gymnasts.'

Before long, the Lincston Gymnastics Club found themselves in a coach heading for the modern part of Heldenstadt. The buildings here were newer and the roads wider. Gilly could see big stores, more open spaces, and a large number of buses and trams. She resolved to be careful crossing roads here as the traffic moved on the right-hand side of the road, of course, and not on the left as it did in Britain.

The coach swooped in to the parking lot of a large sports centre. The Lynx girls disembarked and went through a side door into one of the largest sports halls Gilly had ever seen. You could play a football match in here, she thought in amazement.

The club had arrived a bit early, so they joined the

many spectators who had crowded in to watch the visiting countries as they practised. In the middle of the hall, a boys' group was giving a spectacular display with trampettes – little trampolines – and vaulting horses.

'Know something?' called Deirdre Nicholson so the whole club could hear. 'Those lads are Brits! Aren't they good!'

'Tell you something else,' shouted Sarah Summers back to her, 'it's the Woodfield Eagles! And there are our boys!'

With a thrill, Gilly looked closely at the two lines of boys which were crossing each other at speed. The boys were soaring in the air with split-second timing from the trampettes and somersaulting high over the horses, missing each other by centimetres. Sure enough, she could see her friends – friends such as Sean O'Connor, Rob Wilson, Pete Mactear and Michael Evans – hurling themselves about, too, all part of the display.

'Ooh!' she groaned as Michael, who was known as Lofty because he was so small, finished off the routine with a tail-end Charlie bounce off a trampette to do a handstand on the upright arms of the biggest gymnast.

Their practice over, the boys moved off to enthusiastic applause to join the spectators, the Lynx members waving cheerfully to the girls. Magic, thought Gilly as she and the club dance team took their turn on the floor and began to warm up. They're so good. I hope we get a chance to chat with them later . . .

But there was nothing magic about their dance routine. Everything which could possibly go wrong did so. Some girls forgot their movements, others invented ones. Many of the team did not perform in time to the music. There was a lack of sparkle and the whole piece dragged as if the girls were half asleep.

Natasha Oakley was in despair. At the end of the

session, she told the girls: 'I have never seen such a shambles. You will be laughed at from one end of Heldenstadt to another if you produce a routine like the one you've just done. Tomorrow, you must make a real effort. Or else we may have to quit.' She walked away, her usual high spirits drooping.

In a depressed and silent mood, the team gathered their kit together and sat down to pass time before they had to board their coach. Gilly thought angrily: fancy coming all this way to do a hotchpotch number like that. She slumped, downcast, waiting for the next group to appear.

To her surprise, the next squad were the Bucanians, who arrived late in their dark blue and red tracksuits carrying their balls and hoops. Sonia Krasna clapped her hands to get attention and called out to her team who in turn began to warm up individually.

Gilly saw that Lenka was on her own, by a doorway with her string bag of white balls close beside her. I'll go and have a word, she decided to herself. She got up and went across the floor to the Bucanian girl who was stretching her arms and shoulders.

But as she approached her friend, Vaclav Zoulok appeared from nowhere and stood menacingly between her and Lenka.

'I just wanted to . . .' She faltered with fright as Zoulok raised his arm in a threatening manner. His twisted grin seemed even more scary.

Before she realized what was happening, the four Lynx boys had dashed across the floor and were closing in on the Bucanian.

'Don't you even think of doing anything to our Gilly,' growled Sean. 'Or we'll have your guts for handguards.'

Zoulok backed away, hate etched on his face. Lenka gave Gilly a big wink and the Lynx girls laughed and cheered. The other Bucanians ignored them and carried on warming up.

'Come on, Gill,' said Rob, 'you better keep away from this charming lot – certainly for the moment.'

The boys escorted her back to the team, promising to come over to the Academy one evening to see them. Feeling shattered, she thanked the boys for their timely help. Then the club were called to their coach without a chance of seeing the Bucanians or anybody else perform their display.

Back at the Academy, Gilly soon felt better even though she was still upset about their routine. Christine whirled her into the gym and the brief period of training helped to relax her in mind and body.

After supper, Trudi appeared. For once, she was not dressed in her light green tracksuit but in a pink blouse and skirt. 'Come on,' she said briskly to Gilly and Marcia, 'we're going to the Schloss. Remember? In a few minutes.'

The girls ran upstairs to change into similar clothes. 'What about Lenka?' asked Marcia as she brushed her hair quickly.

'I'll have a look,' said Gilly. She went to the door of their room and looked across the landing. The Bucanians' door was closed. Plucking up all her courage, Gilly knocked and stood there trembling.

The door was flung open by Tereza Srot who glared at Gilly. Behind her, the gymnasts sat on their beds and stared through the doorway.

But Lenka got up. 'I cannot come tonight, Gilly,' she called. 'But I will talk later – ' Srot snorted and slammed the door.

'Well, you've certainly tried hard enough with those creeps,' said Marcia as they went downstairs. 'I'd give them a rest for now.'

'I can't understand why we can't talk to Lenka – or any of the other Bucanians,' pondered Gilly. 'There must be a very good reason. Otherwise, there's no point in them coming to the *gymnaestrada* just to keep to themselves.'

At the bottom of the stairs they found Trudi. With her was a thin young man in a grey uniform with a cap on his head.

'Good!' called Trudi. 'Now we can go. Benno has come to get us.'

To the amazement of Gilly and Marcia, Benno led them through the archway to a large shining smart car. 'Please. In here,' he said.

'What luxury!' said Marcia in wonder as they climbed in the back.

'Benno works for Maria's father, Herr Reinhard Ettlin,' explained Trudi as they drove off at high speed.

'*Herr? Ettlin?* I thought he would be Count Löwenherz.' Gilly was puzzled.

Trudi explained. '*Nein.* No, the Löwenherz title descends from mother to daughter. And Maria's mother is dead. Herr Reinhard is a business man – a successful business man. But because he married a Löwenherz, he can live in the Schloss.'

The car tore along unfamiliar streets and in no time at all reached the hill on which the castle was perched. It wound up a narrow, walled road above the lights of the city and came to a stop in a small, dimly-lit courtyard surrounded by four towers joined by low, stone-built buildings.

Maria was waiting for them. '*Guten Abend!* Good evening! But where is Lenka?'

Gilly explained that the Bucanian minders seemed to be preventing their gymnasts from seeing anybody.

Maria sighed. 'That is a pity. I would like to show her the Schloss, too. Another time, perhaps. Come, I will give you a quick tour.'

As they went through a doorway, she explained that

43

the castle was in effect a museum for the city and that she and her father lived in just one tower. In earlier days, the castle was often under attack from enemy soldiers.

Both Gilly and Marcia found their tour very interesting. Maria led them into vast kitchens with enormous cooking ranges and huge chimneys. She showed them an armoury filled with spears, swords and armour. They passed through a banqueting hall and saw several bedrooms, some the size of tennis courts, with panelling and immense beds.

'Take a bit of time to dust, I should think,' said Marcia.

'You are right,' Maria nodded. 'A small army of cleaners has to work here all the time. And now I will show you the Löwenherz chapel.'

She led the way into a small chapel lit by concealed lighting. It, too, contained panelled walls which were richly decorated with pictures of saints.

But to Gilly, the main feature of interest was a large old painting on the left of the altar. It showed a tall, elegant woman in majestic robes standing in what seemed like this very chapel.

She's the image of Maria, she thought.

Then she noticed it. The woman was wearing a magnificent jewelled ornament on a gold chain around her neck.

'Löwenherz,' said Gilly softly. 'It's the Löwenherz, the Lionheart crest.'

And so it was. The ornament was the size and shape of a human heart with its outline picked out in sparkling stones. In its centre was a rampant lion set in blood-red jewels.

'You are right,' said Maria. 'That is the Löwenherz Pendant. And she is the most famous Countess Löwenherz of all. She has been dead for 200 years. Countess Hemma saved Heldenstadt and its people from becoming conquered by a ruthless enemy.'

'What happened to the Pendant?' asked Gilly.

'It should be here,' said Maria with a sigh. She showed them what looked like a window on the other side of the altar. It was a glass case, again highly decorated with gilded flowers, in which there was a panel which sloped backward. The panel was covered with black velvet and had a hollow in its centre. 'Come, I will tell you the story.'

Maria took her friends to a massive sitting room where she gave them tea and delicious little pastries. She then told the story of her renowned ancestor.

Countess Hemma was the ruler of the region around Heldenstadt which was almost like an independent country within the old Austrian empire. But the neighbouring state, which is now Bucania, tried to take the region over. For many years, there were battles and bloodshed. At one time, Heldenstadt itself was overrun by the enemy.

It was then that the Löwenherz Pendant disappeared. Against many odds, Countess Hemma rallied her people and after a bitter struggle they drove the invaders out. But there was still no trace of the Pendant which had been a stirring symbol of courage. Nor was there for many years.

'But it did turn up!' Marcia interrupted.

Trudi broke in. 'Yes – in Grodnik! It is in the State Museum. But Bucania, they will not return the Pendant to Heldenstadt. We ask them many times, but they say no, no, no because it is theirs by right!'

Gilly began to understand. 'So that's why there is so much bad feeling between you and them. That's why the Bucanians are unpopular with many people here. But why have they been asked to the *gymnaestrada*?'

Maria was about to say more when a door opened. A distinguished-looking man came in with, to their surprise, Fritz Rainer.

Maria jumped up. 'This is my father. You know Herr Rainer, of course.'

When Maria's father had greeted the girls, he said: 'Benno is taking Fritz home now. Perhaps these young ladies would like to go with them.'

Gilly saw with a start that it was getting late. So she, Marcia and Trudi gratefully said yes and got to their feet.

On their way to the car, Maria said to Gilly: 'I think Fritz may have brought some good news. But I will tell you next time.'

After warm thanks and goodbyes, the car took the girls back to the Academy where they arrived to the friendly envy of many of their clubmates.

'It's been quite a day,' yawned Gilly as she and Marcia eventually climbed the long flight of stairs to bed.

But their day was not over yet. On one of the landings, a little figure darted out of the shadows. 'Gilly?' It was Lenka, panting rapidly.

'Lenka – at last! Come and have a chat.'

'No – no time. Please help me. Look after these. Always have them with you. Promise! *Please!*'

To Gilly's astonishment, Lenka thrust her string bag of white balls into her hands and then darted off ahead of them upstairs.

Chapter 5

'Wake up, you lazy lot! Shake a leg!'

Gilly opened an eye lazily. Christine had dashed into their room to make sure that no one would sleep in late that morning.

'Come on,' she called as she shook Shani Patel and Melanie Wood. 'We've got a vital practice – it's an early one! And there's the opening ceremony later.' She ran down the room. 'We've a lot to do and not much time. So I want everyone downstairs – chop chop!'

Marcia grunted and buried herself further down in her bed. She was immediately spotted by their coach. 'Marcia Cherry – you slugabed! You're just the one fathead who could wreck our entire display! Now get up!'

Marcia grumbled and emerged slowly. Then she grinned when she saw Gilly and her friends laughing at her.

'Okay, Christine,' she said. 'I won't be a tick.' She jumped up and reached out for her leotard, as the other girls were.

When Gilly was dressed and had tidied her bed, she noticed the bag of balls which Lenka had given her. I can leave them here, she thought, and tucked them under her bed.

But in the hall, eating a roll and marmalade, she remembered that Lenka had begged her to keep the balls with her the whole time. I better bring them, she decided. It would be awful to lose them. She looked around the hall for the Bucanians, but they were not there.

John came in and made a few announcements. Then he said: 'Our coach goes in five minutes. Please make sure you don't miss it.'

Gilly ran upstairs to collect Lenka's string bag. Leaving their room, she noticed that the Bucanians' door was slightly open and she could hear what sounded like a big row from inside.

What's going on? she wondered. Let's have a quick look-see.

She tip-toed to the door and carefully peeped around it. She was totally startled at what she saw. All the Bucanian gymnasts were standing in a line by their beds

48

and Sonia Krasna was arguing heatedly with Zoulok and Srot.

But it was what the minders were up to which shocked Gilly. They were searching all the bags and suitcases which belonged to the gymnasts and throwing clothes, shoes, and kit on to the floor. They had nearly finished and they were in a very fierce mood, tongue-lashing each gymnast after their inspection. Some of the younger girls were shaking with fear.

What louts, thought Gilly. But they can't have found what they're looking for. I wonder if I can do anything . . .

'Gilly!' Marcia's voice floated up the stairwell. 'Hurry up! We're leaving!'

Gilly hesitated, and then ran down the stairs. She was the last Lynx gymnast to board their coach and earned a look of disapproval from John as she sat down with Marcia. Caroline Mayhew smirked at her lateness.

'Why on earth have you got those wretched balls?' asked Marcia as the coach started off. 'You don't have to do exactly as Lenka asked you. I bet you'll find that bag a real drag.'

'Well, it's because Lenka was so worried,' said Gilly. 'Anyway, she may want them back this evening. By the way, talking of the Bucanians, guess what I saw.' She told Marcia of the search she had witnessed.

Marcia was as perplexed as she was. 'What's up with that mob! Poor kids! They certainly aren't enjoying their stay in Heldenstadt, are they?'

Half an hour later, the 48-strong Lynx group and their coaches arrived at their practice arena, a different one from the sports hall they had used the day before. It was a converted skating rink and like the other venue was filled with spectators who wanted to see all they could of the visitors' displays, practice or not.

Ahead of Lynx was a brilliant acrobatic team from Japan. Gilly and Marcia watched open-mouthed as 22 Japanese men built themselves carefully and daringly into a four-man high pyramid, almost touching the lights of the rink. Then, with gasps from the spectators, the pyramid collapsed like a house of cards expertly on to thick crashmats.

Then it was the turn of Lynx to practise. Fingers crossed, said Gilly to herself as she took off her tracksuit after warming up. We just can't repeat that muddle of yesterday.

To everyone's relief, their routine showed a great deal of improvement. The girls were now working as a team and not as individuals as they had on the previous day. Gilly's tumbling run, ending in her full twisting back somersault, was her best ever and earned some spirited applause from the audience.

Natasha Oakley was pleased. 'Much, much better,' she beamed. 'With a bit of style and polish, we'll have something presentable for our first display. That's tomorrow afternoon, by the way. But we do have a last practice in the morning. Let's aim to do our best, whatever we do!'

When the team returned to the Academy in the late morning, there was enough time for Gilly to train for half an hour in the gym with Christine.

'If you keep that standard of tumbling up,' said Christine, 'you'll be all right at Wembley. But you must spend some more time on the beam.'

Gilly realized that Christine was trying to bolster her hopes. She knew that she was a long way off her best form, but still – some of her old confidence was starting to return.

When she left the gym, she met Marcia with Trudi and Maria. They were waiting to take her out during the hour left before they all went to the opening ceremony of the *gymnaestrada*.

'Come and have a Eiskaffee with us,' urged Maria. 'You must be thirsty after your morning's work.'

So Gilly found herself sitting with her friends outside a coffeehouse consuming cold coffee with ice cream, whipped cream and biscuits.

'Scrummy,' said Marcia, getting whipped cream on her nose. 'Wish they had this at the Moo Moo Milk Bar in Lincston.' For once, she did not mention the bag of balls which Gilly still carried.

'Delicious,' agreed Gilly. 'What a lovely idea to come here.' A thought then clouded her face. 'Wish Lenka could have come with us. She's quite a character. But what a time she's having!'

Licking her spoon, she told Maria and Trudi about the Bucanian minders searching their gymnasts after breakfast. 'Have you seen them today?'

'No,' replied Maria. 'But I have to carry their country's name on a banner at the opening ceremony. Certainly, all's not well with them. I just hope they don't decide to leave the *gymnaestrada* and go back home.'

Trudi said with a smile: 'Me, I am carrying the banner for the British. They will all be at the opening ceremony, Bucanians or not. Which is why we must get going now.'

The girls paid for their refreshments with Austrian schillings and hurried back to the Academy to get ready for their long afternoon.

The City Stadium was packed with thousands of people who had come to see the opening events of the *gymnaestrada*. The gymnasts taking part entered the stadium in large groups representing the 25 nations there.

The Lincston Gymnastics Club marched in with the 200 gymnasts of the British contingent behind a huge Union Jack carried by a British official. The contingent was led by Trudi Kessler who struggled valiantly with a heavy, wide banner which announced GROSSBRITANNIEN. Every now and then, a gust of wind would take her by surprise, and she had to brace herself in case she dropped it.

As a large brass band thumped out stirring music, the delegations formed up in front of the main stand where the Burgermeister, the mayor, of Heldenstadt was waiting to declare the *gymnaestrada* open. Each country received a burst of generous applause and cheering as they marched past the spectators.

Gilly could see many of the banners as she stood waiting for all the countries to arrive. Holland, Switzerland, Sweden, Norway, Denmark, Japan, West Germany, Belgium, Kuwait – they were just some of the countries there. She felt proud to be there with her own nation.

But the one country she was looking for did not appear to have come into the stadium. Bucania. Where were they? In a few minutes, the last country, the host country Austria would be marching on. If the Bucanians did not enter now, they would miss the ceremony. Or had they really decided to pack it in and go home, as Maria had thought?

Her thoughts switched to Lenka's white rubber balls. Without thinking, she had brought them with her on the coach. With a shock, she had then realized that she could not bring them with her into the stadium.

But as they got off the coach in the stadium car park, she suddenly saw Benno, their driver of the night before. He was polishing the bonnet of the luxurious car in which she had ridden to the Schloss. Herr Ettlin must have come to the stadium to watch the ceremony.

Gilly rushed up to the chauffeur. 'Benno! Please keep these for me!' she begged, holding the string bag out to him.

52

Without a word, Benno nodded, took the balls and put them inside the car. Gilly had dashed away gratefully to take her place in the ranks of the British. Now she was waiting to see what had happened to Bucania.

Without warning, a large gap grew behind the gymnasts of the United States. It was a gap which should have been filled by the Austrian contingent. All heads turned towards the entrance to try and see what was happening. The band faltered – and then carried on. Some marchers were coming in.

Loud boos and catcalls from the crowd told Gilly that the Bucanians had at last arrived. Gilly caught glimpses of Maria Löwenherz with her banner, almost in tears; of Sonia Krasna, white-faced and head erect; and of Lenka Zaveska, marching proudly in defiance of their rude welcome.

Only the entry of the Austrians after them quietened the jeers of the spectators who broke into excited cheering and clapping at the gymnasts of their own nation.

Maria said afterwards: 'That horrible Zoulok and Srot, they wanted their gymnasts to return to Bucania. But Sonia Krasna – she argued with them. She telephoned the president of Bucania, and those disgusting brutes, they soon knew that Sonia was very important. So the Bucanians came to the ceremony . . . late. But that's better than not coming at all.'

The ceremony continued with the Burgermeister declaring the *gymnaestrada* open. Then there was folk dancing and music displays, followed by the release of hundreds and hundreds of balloons which filled the sky over the stadium with colour. Finally, a big *gymnaestrada* flag was raised up a pole for the duration of the festival.

Gilly was thrilled to be part of the ceremony and part of the huge family of gymnasts who had come to Austria. For the first time, she realized that the great popularity of

53

her sport went far beyond the competitive side of it. She and Marcia exchanged happy glances.

Back at the Academy, the fun continued. Maria announced that her club would present an Austrian evening, 'a kind of party'. Eveyone must come and take part. The Swedes and British were delighted to accept. But to everyone's disappointment, the Bucanians refused to come, staying in their room away from the entertainment.

Gilly suddenly remembered the white balls which she had given to Benno. She knew they would be safe, but she began to worry whether she should have tried to find the chauffeur at the end of the ceremony.

But while she was changing into a frock, Judy Ambrose came in to their room. 'Look, Gilly. This guy with a cap gave me these for you.' She handed Gilly the string bag with the balls.

'Those blessed things again,' growled Marcia. 'Just to see them makes me feel edgy.'

Gilly thanked Judy and decided that she could at least conceal the balls better. So she put them in a large plastic bag which was in their room for rubbish. But she still took the bag with her to the evening entertainment, not wanting to let Lenka down.

The evening party was held in the dining hall. The tables were pushed back and loaded with food and drink. A piano was wheeled in from somewhere, and candles lit. Welcomed by their Austrian hosts, the Swedish and British visitors, girls and adults, had one of the best times of their whole stay in Heldenstadt. Gilly and Marcia enjoyed every second of it. It was a party they never forgot.

Gretel Hoffmann sat down at the piano and the Austrian girls started the evening with some delightful folk singing and dancing.

One of the songs Gilly could not get out of her head for the rest of the week was:

Muss i denn, muss i denn zum Städtle hinaus
Städtle hinaus, und du, mein Schatz, bleibst hier!
Wenn i komm, wenn i komm, wenn i wiedrum komm
Kehr i ein, mein Schatz, bei dir!

Must I then, must I then to the city away
City away, and you, my love, stay here!
When I come, when I come, when I come back again
Come back again, I'll return to you, my dear!

Then the visitors began to join in. The Swedish girls presented a slow, graceful country dance. Then Gretel played a lively polka and Gilly found herself spinning around the crowded floor with Trudi.

Natasha Oakley was a great hit; being a former ballet dancer, she performed a small solo based on a lively Cossack dance from her native Russia. Then she and John did some old-fashioned jitterbug dancing which made many people, especially Fritz Rainer, cry with laughter.

The Lynx girls came up with their club song which was based on the spiritual *We shall not be moved*. This, too, was very popular, and all there – British, Austrians and Swedish – boomed out the chorus:

We shall not, we shall not be moved
We shall not, we shall not be moved
L, Y, N, X – the very best, we're Lincston
We shall not be moved

After the last chorus, the Austrian girls provided a disco which went on late into the evening. To Gilly's delight, the boys from their club dropped in to the Academy and they immediately joined the dancing.

'Fabulous!' cried Marcia as she swayed with Lofty Evans.

Gilly was just about to reply when a piercing scream from the stairway froze the dancers with fright. The pulsating music stopped dead.

Outside was a sobbing and trembling Maggie Langdale. Someone had searched her dormitory from top to bottom and had made a fiendish mess. Beds, cupboards and suitcases had been turned upside down and clothes, shoes and pillows – many of them slashed with a knife – had been scattered all over the room.

With a shudder, Gilly realized that danger, too, was a visitor to the *gymnaestrada*.

Chapter 6

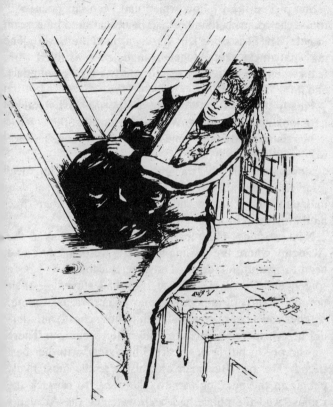

Gilly had the same feeling of horror that she had experienced all that time ago when she and Marcia had first seen the message written in red paint by the vandals on the wall of their club headquarters in Lincston. Then, the message had read: GYMNASTS GET OUT

Now, there was no message, just dreadful untidy chaos

in their room which made her feel that something very private to her had been spoiled. What a terrible end to a perfect evening, she thought.

She picked up a pillow which had been cut open. All round the room, belongings had been scattered in a great jumble. The girls stood still, gazing around them, wondering what to do next. Maggie Langdale's eyes filled with tears when she found her mascot teddy bear ripped apart and flung into a corner.

Finally, Gilly said, 'Well, there's no use just standing here looking at this mess. We had better tidy up.'

Marcia nodded in agreement. 'Come on, gang. This lot won't put itself away.'

Slowly and silently, the girls began to sort out their jumbled clothes. By the time they had finished, it was midnight, and Christine and Natasha came upstairs like mother hens to fuss them into bed.

Next morning, Gilly learned that all the rooms in the Academy where the visiting gymnasts were sleeping had been turned upside down. Only the Bucanians had been spared and that was because they had stayed in their dormitory and not joined the fun of the previous evening.

'I bet you a penny to a pound that those ghastly minders did it,' whispered Marcia to Gilly after breakfast. There was no proof, but in her heart Gilly agreed with her best friend. The two Bucanian officials were the most likely people in the building to have the nerve to ransack the rooms. And the police had been watching the Academy to make sure that people unfriendly to the Bucanians, or even to the British and the Swedes, did not slip in to cause trouble.

'What about the police?' John asked Fritz Rainer. 'Do we tell them?'

Fritz thought for a moment. 'No. I think not. Stories in

the newspapers would not be good for the *gymnaestrada* nor for our visitors.'

Fritz had another worry. The intruder, or intruders, had not only raided the dormitories where the Swedish girls slept but also slashed open the red and blue plastic balls which the Swedes were using in their rhythmic gymnastics display. Fritz had to search far and wide for more balls, and in the end had to borrow some from a club on the other side of the city.

As Gilly waited with the Lynx team to board the coach which would take them to their final practice, she looked at the three large balls she was carrying for Lenka. Why should anyone want to use a knife on rhythmic balls as well as all the other kit, she wondered. She pulled out one of the balls to look at it.

Suddenly, she had a cold, creepy sensation as if someone unpleasant was standing behind her. She whirled around. There, on the other side of the entrance hall, stood Vaclav Zoulok, staring at her with a look of intense hate, made more frightening by his twisted lip.

His eyes narrowed as they passed over her features, her tracksuit, and the bag of balls. He took a step towards her. Gilly, quaking, began to move away.

Marcia, who was chatting nearby with Deirdre Nicholson, sensed that Gilly was worried. She moved over to her friend. 'What's up, Gill?' Then she saw the hunched shape of Zoulok approaching them.

'Push off, Prince Charming!' she barked. 'Just leave us alone!'

Several Lynx heads turned to see what the commotion was about, and some girls began to laugh.

Zoulok halted, enraged. He opened his mouth angrily as if he was going to shout back, but just then a clatter of feet and low voices on the stairs told everyone that the Bucanian team were coming down to go to their practice.

Zoulok stood aside to let the girls pass through the hall, beckoning them impatiently to hurry up, and glancing in fury at Gilly and Marcia.

The last Bucanian was Lenka Zaveska. When she saw Gilly holding one of her white balls under Zoulok's glaring look, she stopped, startled and white-faced. Angrily, Zoulok gestured towards the front door, yelling at her.

As the little gymnast scuttled out, followed closely by the fuming Zoulok, Gilly called to her: 'Everything's fine, Lenka! See you later!' Lenka answered with a cheerful wave before she was shooed on to the waiting coach.

'That bloke's a right nutter!' declared Marcia. 'And a dangerous one, if you ask me. You okay?'

'Fine, thanks,' said Gilly, still feeling a little shaky. She put the ball back in the black bag.

'Do you still have to take those crazy balls with you?' Marcia was in despair. 'We're not even rhythmic gymnasts!'

Gilly nodded determinedly. I'm not going to let Lenka down, she told herself. I'm keeping these balls with me until she wants them.

Just then, John came through the front door. 'Right!' he called. 'Let's get the show on the road! Our coach is here!'

For their final practice, the coach took the Lynx team to a large gymnasium built alongside a swimming pool. Gilly could hear the shouts and splashes of the swimmers as she took her place in the club dance formation in the middle of the floor. At the end of the gymnasium, she could see the Bucanians warming up, their hoops and balls in an untidy pile. As always, the practice session here had attracted many spectators who were attempting to see as much as possible of the *gymnaestrada*, rehearsal or real performance. Among them, she could see Maria

60

and Trudi in their light green tracksuits. She began to feel a lot more cheerful. I wonder how Lenka is, she asked herself . . .

'Gilly!' cried Natasha Oakley. 'Yes, Gilly, you! You seem miles away. Come on! This is no time for anyone to be dozy!'

Blushing, and knowing that Caroline Mayhew was smirking at her, Gilly willed herself to think of nothing but her part in the display. We've got to, *all of us* have got to do well, she thought.

But from the moment their music started, the Lincston Gymnastics Club knew that this practice performance was going to be a good one. The opening slow movements, the following exercises, the dance sequences, the tumbling – all went effortlessly and expertly as the girls not only got their presentation right but also showed that they had fun doing it.

The audience responded with a hearty burst of applause. Trudi and Maria jumped to their feet and waved to the team with enthusiasm.

'We've finally got our act together,' Gilly whispered happily to Marcia as they left the floor.

'Let's hope we can keep it together,' Marcia whispered back.

Natasha glowed with pleasure. 'Girls, not bad, not bad! If you can do that in the official performances – well, I think we can do very well in this *gymnaestrada*. Now there are one or two things we must think about – things to make the routine even better . . .'

'Natasha!' Gilly broke in, almost squeaking with indignation. 'That woman! That awful Bucanian! She's looking at our kit!'

Their choreographer turned around quickly. Gilly was right. While the Bucanian gymnasts were carrying on with their warm-up, Tereza Srot was calmly searching the tracksuits and bags of the Lynx girls which they had placed below the seating along the side of the gymnasium. With a gasp, Gilly saw that the squat Bucanian had found her black bag containing Lenka's three balls and was peering into it.

Natasha jammed her hands on her hips. With a piercing voice which silenced the whole gymnasium, she yelled at Tereza Srot in a foreign language the meaning of which was very clear. Tereza tried to answer back, but was shouted down by Natasha amid growing laughter from the spectators. Finally, flashing looks of hatred, she put Gilly's bag down and slunk back to the end of the gymnasium to join the Bucanian team.

'Must be Russian, that lingo,' said Marcia, remembering that Natasha was Russian-born. Gilly was relieved, for if the Bucanian minder had taken the balls, she had no way of knowing that Lenka would ever see them again. The balls were obviously highly important to her friend.

Gilly wanted to see the Bucanians perform their routine, so she asked Natasha and John whether they could stay a little longer before going back to the Academy. John looked at his watch, because after lunch their first *gymnaestrada* performance was taking place. But Natasha persuaded him that they should stay to watch their fellow guests.

However, before the Bucanians took to the floor, a group of old men from Norway put on a display of dance exercise. Gilly stood riveted with interest as all the dancers must have been the same age as her grandfather. Even though the pace of their routine was slower, their teamwork was just as good as that of many younger groups.

'Gilly!' Someone whispered in her ear. To her surprise and delight, it was Lenka. But her smile vanished when she saw how pale and tired her Bucanian friend looked.

'Lenka . . .'

The little gymnast interrupted in a low voice. 'I cannot talk now. I will tell you later. Gilly, I am so thankful you are helping us. But there is danger. That Zoulok, that Srot – those pigs, they will do anything to get what they want. Be careful . . . very careful!'

'Zaveska!' A rasping shout rang out. The rotund figure of Tereza Srot was stumping towards them, arms waving. Lenka, her eyes pleading silently, slipped away and ran to join her team-mates who were getting ready for their final practice under the direction of Sonia Krasna.

Poor kid, thought Gilly. I wouldn't like to be with her lot.

But all her sympathy for the Bucanians turned into admiration when they put on their rhythmic gymnastics display. Gilly was to remember it as one of the best moments of the whole *gymnaestrada*.

It was a breathtaking performance, with half the girls working with hoops and the rest using white rubber balls like the ones which Gilly was looking after for Lenka. The routine was a mixture of fascinating, well-planned dance and clever exchanges of the balls and hoops.

At first, the Bucanians, in their blue leotards, danced slowly and smoothly, like classical ballet dancers. Then, taking their audience by surprise, the girls transformed the routine into a jazzy dance number. How they managed not to drop any hoops or balls, Gilly could not imagine. Skill, inventiveness, entertainment – the display had it all and everyone in the gymnasium responded by clapping excitedly.

'Just amazing, that was,' said Marcia in the coach going back to the Academy for lunch. 'I can see why rhythmics could be a very popular sport. All that dance – and hoops and balls, too.'

'Well, RG's almost a national sport in countries like

63

Bucania and Bulgaria,' said Gilly. 'And you can do it to
an older age than you can in the gymnastics we do on
apparatus. That's because it's not such hard going physic-
ally. But Lenka and her mates – they were superb! No
one could boo them for that. Of course, they don't only
use balls and hoops. I bet they're just as good with their
clubs. Or ribbons or ropes.'

After lunch Gilly decided to write a postcard to her
family before the club set off to the sports hall for their
display. So she went upstairs to their room and sat on her
bed.

> I'm having a smashing time (she wrote), making good
> friends and seeing interesting places like the castle on
> this postcard. Our routine isn't bad now and our first
> performance is today. I hope you are all well. See you
> very soon.
>
> Lots of love, Gilly xxx

Our first performance, she thought. I can't possibly
take the balls along to the sports hall, they'll be right out
of my sight while we do our routine. What can I do with
them?

Thinking hard, her eyes roamed around the room.
Then they stopped. The rafters, she realized, that's the
answer. I'll hide them in the rafters.

With the help of a table and a cupboard, she climbed
on to one of the large wooden beams which spanned the
room, carrying the black plastic bag with the balls. From
the middle of the beam, two wooden supports went up to
the sloping roof.

It was easy for Gilly, being a gymnast, to move along
the beam and place the black bag between the supports.
No one's going to spot it there, she decided confidently as
she climbed down.

That afternoon, the Lincston Gymnastics Club returned to the sports hall where they had been for their first practice. This time, however, the hall was packed and bustling with people who had come to watch the official performances of the visiting teams to the *gymnaestrada*. When each team was announced, the gymnasts marched in to music which boomed from loudspeakers. A group of people in blazers sat together as judges to decide which teams were good enough to be considered for the *gymnaestrada* finale on the last evening.

As the Lynx girls waited in their yellow leotards, trying not to feel nervous, Christine, Natasha, Trudi and Maria flitted around them, making sure that everyone was tidy and looking their best.

'Good luck!' called Natasha. 'Just do your best – that's all!'

Finally, the American team ahead of them moved out of the arena and the announcer shouted: 'Lincston Gymnastics Club, Great Britain!'

The music started. Their big moment had well and truly come at last.

Gilly lay in her bed, unable to sleep, her mind tumbling over all the happenings of the day. She could still feel the thrill of doing her best double back somersault so far – safe and secure. The Lynx display, too, had gone very well and had even been given a cheer or two by the spectators. Everyone in the club was feeling very happy and looking forward to their remaining two displays.

Later in the afternoon, she had a brief training session in the Academy gym with Christine, and then had gone with Marcia, Trudi and Maria to look at some shops and buy presents for her family. They had ended up in a coffee house by the canal in which coloured lights were reflected. Maria had introduced her to strudel, the famous

Austrian pudding, and she had chosen a delicious one made with fruit and nuts.

Now she was still too excited, her thoughts stopping her from falling asleep. Around her in the dark, her friends were all silent and breathing deeply. She closed her eyes and curled up, trying to relax, trying to drift away into sleep.

Suddenly, she was wide awake. What was that? It sounded like the door handle turning. She listened carefully, but could hear nothing else. I was just imagining it, she told herself, closing her eyes again.

But then a loud creak of a floorboard made her body go rigid. There *is* someone in here, she realized, prickles of fear running down her back. Definitely someone – someone who at this time of night could be up to no good at all.

Chapter 7

Trembling, Gilly slowly opened an eye. At first, there was
nothing to see but darkness. Then, to her horror, a
torchlight flashed on. The beam travelled slowly over the
beds of the sleeping gymnasts on the other side of the
room. Then it crossed over to the beds in the row where
Gilly was lying.

As the beam came closer to her, she closed her eye, trying not to breathe quickly in panic and hoping that the intruder would not notice that she was awake. She prayed in silence: *Please, please get out of here*.

Again, there was nothing to hear. Whoever it was, she thought, must be standing there, shining the torch all round the dormitory. She summoned all her courage and opened her eye again. She was right. The torch light was sweeping carefully into dark corners of the room and over the tops of the cupboards and shelves.

Then, in the chilling silence, the torch suddenly shone upwards and began to search the roof space, moving along the rafters and beams. With a sinking heart, Gilly realized what was going to happen. The bag of balls was going to be discovered.

Fascinated, she watched the ray of light glide along the beam at the end of the room. Then it moved to the beam on which Gilly had climbed the day before. In an instant, the torch had found the bag between the supports and, like a spotlight in a theatre, shone on it so that the black plastic glistened. After a few seconds, the light clicked off and the mysterious visitor slipped out of the room.

Gilly almost sighed aloud with relief. But at the same time, she was even more worried than before. Whoever the person was had obviously been looking for the bag of balls. Now, having succeeded, he or she would slip into the room later and take the bag away.

It took her a long time to get to sleep after that scary happening but she finally succeeded from sheer tiredness.

When she woke, the last girl in the room to do so, she felt dazed and heavy-headed. Around her, her friends bustled about, getting dressed and ready for breakfast. Her eyes shot up to the beam. The bag was still there. Thank goodness, she thought. But I must get it down from there as soon as I can. I wish I didn't feel so worn out, though.

'Come on!' cried Marcia, full of bounding high spirits. 'There won't be anything left to eat if you don't hurry up.' Then she saw Gilly's face and stopped. 'Hey! You look a bit out of sorts. You okay?'

Gilly yawned and nodded at the same time. 'Fine, thanks. Go on down. I won't be long.'

One by one, the girls hurried out of the room and soon Gilly found herself alone. Slowly and with an effort, she got out of bed. When she was dressed in her tracksuit, she drew in her breath and climbed up to the beam as she had done before. She made her way carefully along to the bag and threw it down on to a bed below.

When she jumped down on to the floor, she washed her hands which were covered with dust, took the bag and ran off for the hall, hoping she would not meet Srot or Zoulok.

Instead, however, she met Sonia Krasna on the stairs. They both stopped and regarded each other solemnly.

She looks as tired as me and she's definitely not a happy lady, thought Gilly, looking at the Bucanian's care-worn but still handsome face.

Sonia Krasna put her hand on Gilly's arm. She glanced quickly down to the black plastic bag. 'Are you Gilly?' she asked in a soft, low voice, speaking English with much the same accent as Lenka had.

Gilly answered with a slight nod, eager to exchange at least a few words.

'Gilly, Lenka has told me how you are helping us. Believe me, we are truly grateful. Soon, we hope to explain why things are so difficult for us now. We want to make friends so much. I know you want to, too, with little Laveska and the rest of us.'

Gilly said earnestly: 'Everyone can see that you and

your gymnasts are not being allowed to come near us. It's not your fault. It's those awful officials. I wish they'd go away. I really do.'

'Shh!' Sonia looked hurriedly behind her. The expression on her face showed that she was afraid that someone might hear.

Gilly went on: 'And I want to say how marvellous your routine is. It's one of the best I've ever seen. I bet you've made lots of friends here just by doing that. It's really, really great!'

The serious look on Sonia's face finally broke into a radiant smile as she showed her pleasure at Gilly's praise. 'You are so kind to say that!' she cried.

But an indignant snort interrupted them. Looking up, they saw Tereza Srot glaring down over the banisters. Dropping her smile instantly and without another word, Sonia Krasna went on up the stairs. In a moment, Gilly, too, was on her way gloomily downstairs for breakfast.

In the hall, Trudi dashed up to her. 'Hi! There you are at last! Quick, grab some rolls before they all go.' Her voice became worried. 'You look tired today – do you feel all right?'

I must look a complete wreck, Gilly told herself. Aloud she said: 'I didn't sleep very well but I'm okay, thanks.'

John came in to round up the few Lynx girls still sitting in the hall. 'Hurry up, Gilly. It's not like you to be so late. Shani, Sarah, Maggie, we need all of you in the gym for a chat about our display. Come on, then!'

Blushing, Gilly quickly swallowed the remains of a roll, seized the black bag, and followed Shani Patel into the Academy's gym where the whole Lynx team had gathered to hear their coaches speak. Most were sitting on mats and benches. Gilly looked around for Marcia and found her perched on a vaulting box. Marcia gave her a peppermint and they waited for the session to begin.

70

John spoke first. 'I'm glad to tell you that I've received some very favourable comments on our display yesterday. If we can keep up our standards, we could be in line for an invitation to take part in the grand finale. Having said that, I don't want anyone to relax their efforts. We must make our display one of the best in the *gymnaestrada*. You've all put in a lot of work into the routine and no one wants to see it spoiled at this stage by carelessness. So let's keep it going well!'

Marcia nudged Gilly. 'Don't fall asleep! Christine's got her eye on you.'

Christine had indeed. She was looking at Gilly quite severely. Heavens, thought Gilly, I suppose she thinks I look tired, too. Her attention switched to Natasha Oakley who was now talking to them.

'Girls, as John says, we are not doing too badly. But I believe that we could give an even better impression than we are doing. So I want you all to concentrate on your posture – the way you stand – so that you look like dancers whatever you are doing in the routine and not like sacks of potatoes.'

Natasha paused and looked around at all the girls. 'So, at this afternoon's display, you must convey to the audience by the graceful way you move that you, the Lincston Gymnastics Club, are the best club in the *gymnaestrada*. So perform with elegance, work with confidence, and show that you enjoy the routine from beginning to end. That way, you will be remembered not only for an excellent contribution to this festival but also for being first-rate gymnasts.'

Gilly felt a tingle of excitement as she listened, and she knew that many of her friends must be just as thrilled by Natasha's words.

Christine took over. 'Natasha's absolutely right. Therefore, this morning, we're doing some practice to remind

71

ourselves that as we're working as a team, we must all look like a team and feel like a team.'

'Right,' said John, 'that's why we're going to do some marching.'

A murmur of disbelief rippled around the gym.

'*Marching*?' whispered Marcia. 'Why marching? Any idiot can march, for Pete's sake.'

John explained. 'The first time the audience see you is when you march into the arena as a team. If you shamble on, the audience feels from the start that the club's performance will match the careless way you came in. In many respects, your entry is just as important as your performance. I know everyone here can march; but this morning we will check for any weak points you have as a team.'

So the Lynx girls found themselves in pairs marching in a long line around the gymnasium at the St Margarethen Academy. They marched to brass-band music which blared through Christine's cassette player, watched in amazement by Trudi and Maria. Gilly and Marcia naturally marched together.

'This reminds me of our time with Miss Olive,' grumbled Marcia. Gilly nearly giggled, remembering their former dance teacher in Lincston who had made their class march so that she could correct their posture.

'Keep quiet, Marcia!' called John. 'Hazel – look to your front, not at me! Maggie, you're out of step! All of you, swing your arms higher! Head up, Judy! Shoulders back, Melanie!'

And so it went on. As well as going around the gym in lines, the girls practised marking time, or marching on the spot. This meant that no one would stand still until everyone in their rows had moved into position on the floor mat before their performance.

Before long, Gilly found that she was enjoying the

practice. Christine was right. Marching certainly made you feel part of a team. But she still felt desperately tired and on edge after last night's frightening event.

Finally, John cried: 'Thanks, everyone! Let's leave it at that!'

Good, thought Gilly, perhaps I can have a nap before this afternoon's display. But as she was leaving the gym with her friends, Christine called her over for a chat.

'Gilly, I've never seen you looking so peaky. There's nothing wrong, is there?'

'No, I just didn't sleep at all well last night.' She wasn't going to let on to Christine about the intruder, certainly not yet.

'Well, you're looking as if you could fall asleep on your feet. The last thing we want is for you to make a nonsense of your tumbling this afternoon. It's one of the best things in the display. By far.'

Then Christine had a good idea. 'Tell you what, why don't you have a brief workout with me now and then lie down in my room before lunch. You'll have some peace, and I bet you'll feel a whole heap better.'

Gratefully, Gilly agreed. And after some body conditioning and some tumbling practice, and not forgetting to bring Lenka's bag with her, she fell asleep on Christine's bed in a little room on the first floor.

When Christine woke her before lunch, she did indeed feel a lot more normal. The heaviness in her head had vanished.

'Good,' said Christine, 'let's hope that little rest has done the trick. Now go and have something to eat.'

In the hall, she joined Marcia, Trudi and Maria and tucked into a plate of dumplings.

'You do look a lot more like your old self,' said Marcia, noticing a vast improvement in Gilly's looks.

The Austrian girls nodded and beamed. '*Ja*,' declared

Maria. 'Yes – how do you say it in English? – you are back on your toes.'

Gilly smiled at her friends. 'Thanks, I really am beginning to feel alive again.'

In the coach on the way to the sports arena for their second official display, Marcia said: 'That Zoulok. I reckon he was looking for you this morning. He was going bananas before lunch, standing at the bottom of the stairs, fussing and making sure he saw every girl who was in the building. You know that Swedish gymnast with fair hair who looks like you from behind? He dashed up to her and seemed very disappointed when he found he had the wrong girl. What a viper that man is.'

Drat, thought Gilly, I wish all this Bucanian business was over. And that reminds me. I've got to get someone to look after this bag while we do the display.

She thought for a few moments. Then she said to her friend: 'I'm going to see Christine.'

She got up from her seat and, taking the bag of balls, found her trainer sitting at the front of the coach with John.

'Feeling all right, now?' asked Christine. 'What can I do for you?'

Gilly showed her the bag. 'Could you please do me a big favour and keep this with you during our display? It means a lot to me. It belongs to a friend and I'd hate to have it stolen.'

Christine looked curiously at the balls and then at Gilly. 'I've noticed you've always got these with you. Now relax. I'll look after this bag if you get that worried look off your face.'

The second display by the Lincston Gymnastics Club at the Heldenstadt *gymnaestrada* was undoubtedly their best. All the girls agreed afterwards that it was the one

74

that they enjoyed performing the most. Everything went right from the moment they marched on to the floor.

The Lynx coaches were also delighted with the way the performance had gone. The praiseworthy result, with the delight shown by the spectators, had proved the worth of all the preparations, all the practices which the club had undertaken.

Natasha hugged every girl she could get hold of, and a happy John and Christine were interviewed by several sports reporters. Sean O'Connor, in his role as a journalist, wrote for the *Lincston Advertiser*:

The yellow leotards of Lynx received tumultuous applause. And well they might. The girls performed with precision and polish, their well-executed performance linking the grace of gymnastics and dance with patterns to music.

As Gilly took back Lenka's bag of balls from Christine, she was both overjoyed and thankful – overjoyed because the club had done so well and thankful because she had recovered enough from her dreadful night's experience to carry out her tumbling almost perfectly. All she wished now was that she could get rid of Lenka's bag.

Christine said to her: 'That was very admirable to pull yourself together like that. I'm beginning to think you might do well at Wembley when we get back. I wish, though, you'd tell me what's troubling you. It certainly shows on your face, whether you're tired or not.'

Wembley? Gilly had almost forgotten about the Junior Champion Gymnast competition. But she was going to wait until next week when she was back home before troubling herself about that. As for telling Christine about the Bucanians – she knew she would have to say something to her coach by tomorrow if nothing happened to end her problem.

That afternoon, Gilly, Marcia and Trudi set off from the Academy for more sightseeing. It would be one of their last chances to do so before they left Heldenstadt.

'You must see St Michael's Cathedral,' said Trudi. 'It is a lovely old place.' So she led them, happily chattering, through a maze of narrow streets and lanes. One of the places they passed through was the main square with the Löwenherz statue in it.

Lionheart. I wish I was lion-hearted right now, thought Gilly as they turned into a small alley. Then I could deal with these three balls once and for all.

Then she stopped dead with fright. Coming down the narrow passageway were Tereza Srot and Vaclav Zoulok.

The grim-faced Bucanians caught sight of the terrified girls and, without a second's hesitation, began running towards them.

Chapter 8

The three girls did not wait to see what the Bucanians wanted. They turned and fled down the alley as fast as they could move.

Gilly knew straight away that the horrible pair could only want to seize Lenka's bag of rhythmic gymnastics balls. Their target could only be her.

'Scatter!' she yelled. Trudi dashed off down a back street to the right. Marcia, her arms and legs pumping hard, carried on ahead. Gilly herself nipped left down a lane where the tops of the buildings nearly touched each other.

Halfway down the lane, she paused and looked behind her. She was right. The Bucanians were after her – her alone. They had turned into the lane and were pounding towards her, Zoulok ahead of Srot.

Gilly started to run again, wondering where to go, where to hide. There were no other people about and no friendly doorways which she could pop into. While, as a gymnast, she was fit and could run for a long time, she could not go on for ever. She knew, too, that she could move faster if she did not have to carry the black plastic bag.

Of the two Bucanians, Zoulok was the one she feared the most. She felt sure that he could not only race ahead of his dumpy partner but also catch up with her.

She glanced over her shoulder. Sure enough, the hunched Bucanian was moving well in front of the panting Srot and was rapidly closing the gap between him and her.

Gilly suddenly found herself in a small square. In the middle was a tall fountain with statues of three mermaids in its middle. On the edges of the square were flower-beds and on the other side, Gilly could see a large, dark church.

Go over there, she ordered herself. So she tore across the square to the other side, feeling spray from the fountain as she passed it. Zoulok emerged from the lane. Then he, too, began to run across the square.

With a shiver, Gilly could almost feel the gloating look which her pursuer gave her. Where next? Desperately, her eyes searched the openings to the square. As a result, she realized that there was only one place she could go where she could not be seen. The church.

Without a backwards glance, she hurried through the big front door into the gloomy interior, lit only by light coming through high stained glass windows. There was no one in the church, and every step she took seemed to echo. She half walked, half ran down the aisle on the left and leaned on the last of the tall pillars which reached into the roof of the church. Clutching the black bag, she closed her eyes, trying not to breathe so heavily.

In a moment, she heard the catch on the church door open with a crack like a pistol shot. The noise could mean only one thing. Zoulok had arrived.

Gilly noticed a side door opposite her pillar. That was the way she must leave the church – if she could get clear of the Bucanian. She turned to face the pillar and moved around so that she could not be seen from the front door, her ears straining to catch any sound.

Before long, she heard footsteps clumping towards her. Panic-stricken, she waited until they were almost on top of her. Then, on tip-toe, she slid around the pillar, trying to keep it between her and Zoulok, and praying that she wouldn't be heard . . . or seen.

Zoulok strode past the pillar and turned into the centre of the church, crossing in front of the altar. He halted at the top of the aisle on the right, listening for any noise which gave Gilly's whereabouts away. He then paced down towards the main door again, stopping to peer into a little chapel set into the wall of the church.

Gilly wondered again: what do I do now? Then, as an answer, the front door banged open and a bunch of tourists, led by a guide, began to enter the church, talking a foreign language in loud, penetrating whispers as they came in. Zoulok turned to watch them, distracted by their chatter.

Gilly saw her chance. She slipped away from the pillar and darted off to the side door, not daring to look behind her. She pushed the door open silently and came out into another narrow side-street. She turned right and hurried away towards the bottom of the street where she could see lots of people walking about.

When she reached the end of the street, she found herself in the middle of a bustling market with stalls stretched out along a bank of the canal. Gilly guessed that this must be what Trudi called the 'flea market', a place popular with visitors to Heldenstadt who wanted to find a bargain in objects such as old books, ornaments, jewellery and paintings.

Gilly also knew that it would be hard for Zoulok to catch her in the crowd let alone see her. She was not sure, however, how she was going to find her friends and get back to the Academy. For the time being, though, she decided to walk through the throng of tourists by the stalls so that she could get as far as she could from the grisly Bucanian.

The stalls were bright and interesting, and Gilly began to find that her attention was being held by the items on view. Her pace slowed, and when she came to a stall of antique dolls run by a little old lady, she stopped altogether to look at the fascinating lace and velvet-costumed display.

'English?' asked the stall-holder.

Gilly nodded yes.

The old lady reached down and showed her a little doll in a green dress with lace trimmings and a straw hat. 'English,' she said with a smile. 'Victorian.'

She's really lovely, thought Gilly. Think of it. She could be one hundred years old.

Just then, some instinct made her look up. With a gasp, she saw Zoulok pushing his way through the crowds towards her. She thrust the English doll back at her elderly owner and once more shot away, around the back of the stall. Zoulok began to run as well.

Gilly realized afterwards she could have called for help from the crowd, but blind panic had made her bolt off again.

She ran along in front of the buildings behind the market, trying to find some way of escape which would let her vanish. Then all of a sudden, she came across a flight of stone steps which led away from the canal. With a sob of relief, she scooted up the steps. But within seconds, she heard Zoulok charging up behind her.

I just can't go on running like this, she cried to herself in despair. Help me, someone! Help!

For once, her silent pleading was rewarded. At the end of the steps was a wall, low enough for her to climb – if she could reach up to the top. It was worth trying. Holding the bag in her teeth with the balls hanging over her shoulder, she leaped with a huge effort, catching hold of the highest bricks. With a grunt, she pulled herself up on to the wall with ease, using the strength she had developed as a gymnast.

She mounted the wall in the nick of time. Zoulok came stumbling up the steps and stood waving his fist up at her. Gilly did not stay to chat. She set off along the narrow top of another wall leading away between the backs of two rows of old buildings just as if she was giving a performance on a beam in a gymnasium. She could hear Zoulok cursing and trying to scramble up and she knew he might succeed before long.

The wall did not take her far. It came to an end after ten metres or so against the windowless side of what looked like a former stable. Gilly had no choice about her next move which was to jump down, but she could decide which side of the wall to dismount. There were lights shining through the two lower windows of the building on her left while on the right the windows were dark.

Going left meant that she would find people. Going right could result in her not being able to get any further. So, decided Gilly, I'll keep to the left.

She jumped down accordingly into a small yard and made her way to a green door set beside the lighted windows. The door was unlocked and Gilly, trembling slightly, went into a short passage which was piled high with cardboard boxes. Ahead of her was another door which was half open.

Gingerly, she pulled the door fully open and found herself in a shop full of china, pottery and glass goods.

A young woman in glasses, about Christine's age, came running over. '*Was ist das*?' she cried in surprise.

'Speak English?' asked Gilly, moving to a chair and sitting down in utter weariness.

'A little,' said the girl slowly. 'Why you come that way? In this shop? That way – that way is private.'

'I'm sorry. A man was chasing me. I am a British gymnast – at the St Margarethen Academy. I came in here by accident.'

'British gymnast? Ah – Heldenstadt *gymnaestrada*! *Ja*?'

Gilly nodded and smiled. Hopefully, this woman would help her.

'What you want? Police? Taxi? Cup of tea?'

I'll settle for a taxi, thought Gilly. That way, I'll get back without hassle and without running across that dreadful Zoulok. 'Thanks,' she said aloud. 'A taxi would be wonderful.'

'Wait. I telephone. You tell the police about that man – later?'

'Yes,' said Gilly. 'Later.' She sat while the girl went to pick up a telephone, watching out for Zoulok in the reflection of a mirror which looked out into the shopping arcade where the shop was situated.

In a minute, the girl returned, a wide smile on her face. 'Ja! A taxi comes!' She explained to Gilly that she had to walk through the arcade to the street where the taxi would collect her. She told Gilly that she would come with her but she could not leave the shop.

Thanking the girl very much, Gilly left after a few minutes and made her way up the arcade past some expensive-looking shops selling handbags, silver, dresses and furnishings. When she reached the street, she waited in the arcade entrance for the taxi, keeping a lookout for the Bucanians. She could see nobody else around.

A car came round the corner and slowed down. It flashed its headlights.

Gilly waved. Here's the cab, she thought. She stepped forward as it drew up and stopped.

Before she could react or cry out, the rear door of the car was flung open. To her utter horror, Tereza Srot sprang out, seized her and bundled her in, bag and all, forcing her down on to the floor. A ghastly laugh told her that Vaclav Zoulok was at the wheel.

The door slammed and the car drove off at high speed through the streets of Heldenstadt.

Chapter 9

The next couple of hours were among the worst of Gilly's whole life.

Her head was pressed down by Tereza Srot below the back seat of the car so that she could not be seen by anyone passing by. She could not move at all without the burly Bucanian hurting her neck.

The floor of the car smelled of oil and sweat and something very unpleasant. It was also very dusty and nose-tickling. Gilly hoped that she was not going to be sick.

At first, she tried to cry 'help!' in case any passerby could hear her. But every time she made a sound, Tereza Srot cuffed her – hard. In the end, Gilly gave up trying to struggle and resigned herself to waiting to see what was going to happen to her.

She could tell nothing from the conversation which the two Bucanians were having. Every now and then, she recognized words such as 'Bucania' or 'Grodnik' which, of course, did not help her to understand what Zoulok and Srot were saying. In any case, she did not think it likely that she could be taken over the Bucanian border without being seen by the guards at the frontier post.

Gilly also realized that Marcia and Trudi would run back to the Academy to tell their coaches and Fritz Rainer that they had been chased by the Bucanian officials. That would probably mean that the Austrian police would be on the look-out for them.

In the meantime, all Gilly could do was to try and guess where they were. At first, it was clear to her that their route was taking them through the centre of the city. She could hear car horns, the spluttering of motorbikes and, occasionally, the squeal of brakes. Sometimes, their car had to stop suddenly at what must have been traffic lights or pedestrian crossings.

In each case when they had to stop, Zoulok muttered with impatience, stamping on the brakes. When they moved off again, he would try for as fast a start as possible, making the engine roar and the car jerk forward. Frequently and without warning, the car would dash away for a few moments and then slow down once more. Gilly guessed then that Zoulok must be overtaking other traffic.

After a while, the car's progress became smoother and its engine settled down to a steady rate. We must have left the city limits, she told herself.

Srot took her hand off Gilly's head and Gilly heard a rustle as the Bucanian bully picked up the black plastic bag. She tried to get up, but received another vicious slap which made her cry silently. The empty bag landed on the floor beside her, and she was aware that her persecuter was looking at the three white balls in their string bag.

Srot gave a low whistle and began to talk quickly with Zoulok. But, from what Gilly could gather, he did not agree.

Where are we going? Gilly asked herself. To the Bucanian border? To a hiding place? All she knew was that she could not carry on much longer curled in her cramped position on the floor of the car.

Then, after what seemed a very long time, the note of the car's engine changed to a higher one as Zoulok began to use his lower gears more. Gilly could also feel that the car was now turning many corners in the road. She immediately realized that they must have reached the mountains overlooking Heldenstadt and that the car was climbing up a steep and twisty road.

Before long, Srot took her hand off Gilly's head and pulled her roughly on to the left-hand side of the seat, probably because she thought that they were in a part of the region where few people would see them.

At first, Gilly felt stiff and dizzy. Then she could see that she was right about being in the mountains. They were driving up a road on the left side of a valley which was covered with fir trees. Across the valley, she could see more forests and in the background, a tall, snow-covered mountain.

On the seat, between her and Srot, lay the string bag holding the three white rhythmic gymnastics balls. Those balls, thought Gilly wearily, have caused me more trouble than I could imagine. They've more-or-less ruined this week for me.

Slowly, Gilly began to feel more normal. In a few minutes, she was able to start thinking hard again. What were they doing in the mountains? What did these dreadful Bucanians want with her?

She had a quick look at Tereza Srot. The beefy Bucanian gave her an evil grin and raised her arm as if to hit her. With a feeling of terror Gilly edged away as far as she could into the corner of the seat. Jeepers, she wondered for the first time, have this revolting lot got it in for me? Her heart began to beat faster.

Halfway up the valley, Srot picked up a map, opened it, and examined it closely. Then she jabbed a stubby finger into the middle of the map and spoke to her partner.

Zoulok disagreed again. He spat out of the car window, shook his head and began to argue, glancing back angrily at Srot.

Gilly put her hand to her mouth in fright. For heaven's sake, she cried silently, keep your eye on the road. You'll drive us all over a cliff.

With a hiss and still shaking his head, Zoulok drove the car into a parking place on the side of the road. He parked the car beside the low metal barrier which ran around the edge of the car park and which separated them from the steep forest-covered slope which fell away to the floor of the valley.

Both Bucanians flung open their car doors and got out. Srot marched around to the front and slapped the map down on the car bonnet, her finger still jabbing away. Zoulok joined her and their voices continued loudly in argument.

Gilly seized her chance. Grabbing the string bag of

balls, she shot out of the car and jumped over the barrier, praying that there wasn't a high cliff on the other side. Thankfully, there was only a three-metre drop and that on to soft ground. She landed on both feet as if she was vaulting, rolled forward once on to her feet again, and dashed down the slope as fast as she could go, slithering and sliding through the thick forest.

As she jumped, she heard Zoulok utter a cry of anger. Then he, too, leaped over the barrier, cursing as he landed heavily. In a moment, she could hear him crashing down through the trees behind her.

Where she was going, Gilly did not know. She just kept running downhill, trying to keep the branches from scratching her, tearing her clothes and, worse, plucking the string bag from her.

The slope began to level out and Gilly knew that Zoulok would soon catch up with her. She came out on to a forest path and was tempted to run down it to the right. But she realized her hopes of escape would be better if she stayed off the path. So she crossed it and continued to hurry downhill.

At the bottom of the valley, the sound of rushing water told her she was coming to a small stream. It also meant that the ground on the other side of the stream would start to rise uphill. She was too exhausted to think of clambering up another steep slope. Where she could go next, she just did not know.

But when she came to the stream, she saw a possible answer. Above the bank on the other side was a large fir tree with many thick branches. She stopped for a moment, but the rustling behind her was a sign that her Bucanian hunter was coming closer.

Gilly made up her mind. She must act now. So she crossed the stream, jumping from stone to stone, and flung the string bag as high as she could into the tree's branches. To her relief, the bag caught on a twig.

She then reached up and caught hold of the tree's lowest branch. From then on, it was easy. As if she was performing on the world's largest set of asymmetric bars, she swung herself up silently and quickly from branch to branch. When she reached the white balls, she did as she had done before earlier that afternoon and held the bag in her teeth.

In a minute, she was out of sight from the ground. Near the top of the tree, she found a branch to perch on. So she sat there panting, hugging the tree trunk with her eyes closed, praying that Zoulok did not hear her climb or, indeed, see her now.

She could still hear the Bucanian crashing about somewhere in the forest on the other side of the stream. For a time there was silence, as if he was listening for Gilly to make a noise. She herself kept motionless.

Finally, after more noisy movement among the trees, Zoulok called out. Srot answered him. After a brief conversation, Gilly heard him make his way slowly up to the car park. Then, after what seemed hours, the sound of the car driving away reached her.

Taking her time, Gilly climbed down from the tree, keeping alert for any noise which could mean that one or the other of the Bucanians was still looking for her. She recrossed the stream, but rather than climb back to the road, decided to follow the forest path down the valley taking the chance that she would meet someone who could help her.

It was now late afternoon, and Gilly realized that she must get a move on so that she would not be caught by darkness when she was still in the middle of the forest. So she set off briskly, looking cautiously into the trees on both sides of the path and glancing behind her in case the horrific shape of Zoulok appeared.

As the shadows of the trees grew longer, so did the valley begin to feel creepy. Gilly wondered whether she had made the right decision; whether she would have been wiser to go back on to the road.

Then she thought she heard something. She stopped to listen closely, but she could not catch any other noise than the rushing of the nearby stream and the wind rustling the trees. She continued on her way, trying not to break into a run.

All of a sudden, she did hear a sound, an unmistakeable sound somewhere ahead of her – the sound of someone chopping wood. Despite herself, she began to run down the path.

Round a bend, she came across one of the most welcome sights she had ever seen. There, hacking intently away at a log with an axe, was a young forester. He was wearing a green Tyrolean hat, as many Austrian men do, with a sprig of red blossom in its band. Behind him was a small green pick-up truck full of tree branches.

The forester looked up in surprise as Gilly staggered up to him, clutching her string bag.

'Telephone?' she asked him with a croak in her voice. Then she collapsed at his feet, totally exhausted.

It was dark by the time Gilly got back to the St Margarethen Academy. She arrived in Heldenstadt as she had left it – by car. But this time she travelled in the luxurious car belonging to Schloss Landskron. When Herr Ettlin had heard what had happened to Gilly and where she was, he insisted on sending Benno and his car to the mountain village where Klaus, the forester, had taken her.

Christine and Gretel Hoffman had travelled with

Benno. Once they had collected the exhausted Gilly from the village *Gasthaus*, or inn, where the motherly landlady was looking after her, the car sped back to the city.

Gilly slept in comfort curled up in a corner of the back seat. The three white balls were placed on the shelf behind her. Christine and Gretel were dying to ask her what had happened to her, but they knew they would hear all her adventures when she was back, rested, at the Academy.

Gilly woke when the car drove into the Academy's gateway, waved in by the police guarding the building. Sleepily, she asked: 'Zoulok, Srot . . . where are they?'

'Don't worry about *them*,' said Gretel. 'They won't ever bother you again. We promise.'

When Gilly got out of the car in the courtyard, she found a group of friends waiting for her. Their worried features broke into smiles when they saw her emerge, still with the string bag. With happy cries of relief, Marcia, Trudi and Maria rushed forward to hug her.

Marcia was trying not to cry. 'Good old Gilly. You're really a hero!'

To her delight, a fourth figure ran up to her to fling her arms around her. It was Lenka, a big grin on her face. 'Thank you, dear Gilly, thank you,' she cried. 'I can now take your burden from you. In a moment, you will see truly what an important duty it was.' She took the balls from Gilly and began to clap her hands. Several other people began to clap, too.

Gilly blushed. She became aware of John, Natasha, Fritz Rainer and Sonia Krasna joining in the clapping. Also applauding her were girls from the Swedish and Bucanian clubs as well as from Lynx. Gilly was thrilled to see the Lynx boys there, too – Sean O'Connor, Rob Wilson, Pete Mactear and Michael Evans.

John came up to her. 'Well done! Three cheers! Gilly –

we're so proud!' he beamed. 'But look. Before you slip off, the police want a quick word with you. Can you spare them a minute or two – right now?'

Gilly looked at Christine, wishing she could get away. But Christine nodded. So Gilly found herself in the hall describing her adventures on the run to Kirstin Vogel, a senior Austrian *Polizistin*, or policewoman. The Lynx coaches, with Fritz, Gretel and Sonia, listened closely, too.

'Thanks. You did so very well,' said Kirstin at the end. 'Now we will catch those thugs and throw them over the border, back into Bucania.'

After patting Gilly on the back, Fritz asked: 'Sonia, will *you* get into trouble? From your government – when you return to Grodnik?'

'No,' said Sonia calmly. 'Those morons will be in disgrace. Big disgrace. They have found nothing here. Or proved anything. And they have kidnapped a young girl in another country. Now we must explain all this business to you.' She beckoned to Lenka.

Lenka was the centre of attention in the hall, surrounded by the adults and a small group of friends. Missing was Maria, who had to return to her castle home.

What's going on? Gilly wondered. Lenka had a sharp knife in her hand and her three white gymnastics balls on the table in front of her.

When Lenka saw Gilly, she called out: 'Gilly, this is why you were carrying such big worries around with you – big worries for us all.'

In silence, Lenka examined the balls carefully, finally selecting one. She then grasped the knife and plunged it into the ball. She slit it open carefully, and from inside it, pulled out what seemed a bunch of dark rags. With all eyes on her, she unwrapped an object which immediately glowed and sparkled in the lights of the hall.

In amazement, no one stirred, their eyes fixed on the glittering reflections of many blood-red jewels.

Then Gilly saw the outline of the ornament and almost in disbelief she realized immediately what it was.

Lenka broke the silence. With a sob of emotion, the little gymnast told everyone in the hall what Gilly already knew: 'The Pendant of the Löwenherz! This is the Löwenherz Pendant of Heldenstadt!'

Chapter 10

Gilly felt like laughing and crying and getting cross all at once. The staggering news that she, without knowing it, had been carrying around a set of priceless jewels which brought her into very real danger had left her completely numb.

No wonder Lenka had asked her to have the white balls

always with her. No wonder Zoulok and Srot were so interested in them. No wonder the two evil-looking Bucanians had chased her so hard in the city and in the forest for that matter . . .

Was it fair to let her go through all her experiences without telling her? And why pick on her? But what if she *had* known she was carrying around the Löwenherz Pendant like a pocket handkerchief? Perhaps she would have let someone else take over the responsibility. And what then? Would Srot and Zoulok have found it easier to grab the Pendant? Many questions whirled through her head – but no certain answers.

Gilly became aware that Sonia Krasna was talking. The Bucanian leader had started to tell the story of how the Löwenherz Pendant was moved from the State Museum, Grodnik, back to its rightful place in the city of Heldenstadt.

'I had never thought much about the Pendant,' said Sonia, her large blue eyes sweeping over her audience who were sitting spellbound. 'I knew about it being in the State Museum, of course. But, like so many people in Grodnik, I never knew that it was so important, so stirring to the people of Heldenstadt. Then I met Fritz Rainer.'

She reached out and put her hand in Fritz's. 'It was at the world championships; twenty years ago in Germany. Then I heard about the Pendant.'

'Yes,' said Fritz, looking at Sonia with a warm smile. 'Even then, we found it difficult to meet and talk. But I told her about the Pendant and why it was so important to our people. She said straightaway that she thought that it should be returned to Heldenstadt.'

Sonia continued. 'But there was nothing I could do at the time and certainly not alone against the authorities in Bucania. Fritz and I did not meet again for some time, but we wrote letters.'

'How romantic!' murmured Marcia dreamily.

Gilly gave her friend a speedy knock with her elbow to keep her quiet.

Fritz explained that eventually both Sonia and he became leading coaches in their countries and this gave them opportunities to meet at big international gymnastics competitions.

Two years ago, they met at a conference in Switzerland which discussed the coming *gymnaestrada* at Heldenstadt. Fritz thought that if Bucania could be invited to the event, it would be a wonderful chance to try again to get the Pendant back from Grodnik. Once more, Sonia and he talked about the possibility.

'The difficulty was,' Fritz went on 'that at first no one in Heldenstadt wanted to ask Bucanian gymnasts to the *gymnaestrada*. People here had disliked Bucania for so long. And the Bucanians themselves did not show any interest in wanting to come. But finally, and with not much time to go, our organization sent an invitation to Grodnik.'

Sonia sighed at the memory. 'Our officials immediately said no. It was impossible to allow any Bucanian gymnasts to go to a *gymnaestrada* in western Europe. But I pointed out that Heldenstadt was so close to Grodnik. We could not keep on for ever staying away from our next-door neighbours. Especially in a sporting event in which we would probably do well. Eventually, they agreed that a small group could go from my club.'

Fritz said, 'To me, it was wonderful news. I know if Sonia had not been so well known in her country, permission to come here would not have been granted. So yet again I wrote to her. I asked her if she could do anything about what I called "the heart of the matter". I did not want to mention the Pendant by name. That was in case someone working for the government got hold of the letter.'

Sonia took up the story. 'I knew that, because permission for us to go to Heldenstadt was so slow in coming, no one in the Government would even dream of allowing us to take the Pendant with us. So we had to find some other way of getting it out of the State Museum. What's more, we had to move quickly as we were due to go to Heldenstadt within a few days.'

She related how she talked with some trusted friends in the Dynamo Club who agreed that the Pendant rightfully belonged to their neighbours across the border. Before long, Sonia and her friends had an answer – perhaps the only answer – to the problem. They would steal the Löwenherz Pendant from the State Museum, Grodnik.

Steal it! Gilly was flabbergasted. But how . . .? She caught the eye of Lenka who burst into giggles which she immediately tried to stifle.

Sonia stopped her story and turned to the little gymnast. 'Zaveska, when you have finished making a fool of yourself, you might perhaps tell us what happened next.'

Lenka wiped her eyes, paused for a moment, and then described what Gilly thought was one of the most exciting parts of the whole affair.

Because of its fame, the Pendant was displayed by itself in a small room in the State Museum. It was on view in a glass case with small spotlights shining on the jewels to make them sparkle. The case was not difficult to get into because it had no locks. But the main hitch was that the case was set back out of reach behind a tall metal grille which stretched up to the ceiling. There was also an armed guard in the room.

'But,' said Lenka, her eyes shining with excitement, 'there was a small gap between the top of the grille and the ceiling. We thought there was room for a small person

97

to squeeze through. The small person would also have to be strong enough to climb the grille – two times. Once to get in. Once to get out. So – who did we want? A small gymnast.' She paused again and blushed.

'You!' cried Gilly. 'They chose you for the job!' There was a hum of admiration around the hall.

Lenka nodded. 'I had to climb up. When everything was ready.'

Sonia took over the story again. 'We decided to make lots of noise in the room next door. We hoped that the guards would come to stop us and so the Pendant would be left alone for a few moments. It was all a huge gamble. To lose would have meant jail for many of us. That morning – that morning is one I shall never forget.'

Nor will many people who were on duty at the time at the State Museum. Early that morning, before many tourists arrived, a group of young people, boys and girls who looked like students, came to the Museum with their leader. She was a striking-looking woman with reddish hair and blue eyes. She led the group through the galleries so that they could see the paintings, statues, photographs and documents which illustrated the history of modern Bucania.

Suddenly, some of the boys in the group began to fight among themselves, yelling and screaming as they did so. Guards and attendants hurried to the scene from all over the Museum to stop the hullabaloo. The other people in the group tried to help but many of them got in the way of the guards.

No one saw a small girl and a tall boy from the group slip into the nearby room where the Löwenherz Pendant was on view. The boy gave a leg-up to the girl at the iron grille protecting the display. Quick as a monkey, she shimmied up the bars and through the narrow gap between the grille and the ceiling. She then slid down the other side of the bars, landing lightly in front of the glass case. She seized the glittering piece of jewellery from the case and passed it between the bars to her companion.

The boy stuffed the Pendant in his pocket and gave her another lift up, this time putting his arms through the bars. He then strolled slowly out of the room, made his way casually to the entrance hall and left the Museum after buying a postcard of the Pendant.

The girl, urged on by fright, squeezed through the gap again and dropped down in front of the grille. The operation had taken less than a minute. In the next-door gallery, there was still the noise of yelling and cursing as the guards tried to halt the rumpus. The girl, too, slipped away and left the museum.

Suddenly the uproar was stopped. The boys who were fighting were taken to the security office to await the arrival of the police.

Then the disturbance was forgotten as the shocked guards discovered that the Löwenherz Pendant, one of the Museum's most famous showpieces, had vanished. The boys were searched and then allowed to go after they had given their names and addresses.

The search was now on throughout Grodnik to find the Pendant and punish its thieves. Above all, the Bucanian authorities did not want the Pendant to be taken across the border and returned to Heldenstadt. There was talk of banning the gymnasts from the Dynamo Club from going to the *gymnaestrada* but that would only draw attention to the loss of the Pendant.

'We were sweating with fear,' Sonia told her listeners who were gripped by every word. 'Our Dynamo group was leaving the next morning for Heldenstadt. At any moment we could be searched before we left the country. But at the time, no one thought that young gymnasts could have stolen the Pendant. Most officials thought a gang of criminals must have done it.'

'Yes,' said Lenka. 'And we were also afraid that someone in the Club would give us away – by accident maybe. My father spent all that night trying to seal the Pendant in a white ball. You know, without any marks showing on the shiny surface. The balls he ruined! But he did it with the last ball.'

Someone whistled with relief.

Natasha asked: 'But that dreadful couple, Zoulok and Srot, how did they get here?'

'It was like this,' said Sonia. 'On the morning we took the train here, some policeman discovered that the boys who started the fight were gymnasts. That started the authorities thinking. Some big boss man then decided that it was worth sending someone to check on the group who had gone to Heldenstadt. So, that charming pair arrived here.'

Gilly shivered as she remembered her adventures with Zoulok and Srot.

Sonia continued: 'Fritz was going to take us up to the castle so we could present the Pendant to its true guardians. But, of course, we could not – thanks to those two thugs. Every move we made was watched. Everything we owned was searched. We were all questioned, questioned. Zaveska had the worst time. As you know, it was she who brought the Pendant to this city.'

Everyone's eyes turned to Lenka. Trudi shook her hands in delight.

'She was interviewed the whole time about the Pendant,' said Sonia. 'She did not help herself by being rude to them. But she decided to get someone else here at the Academy to look after the balls. That was until we ourselves had the opportunity of handing the Pendant over. Zaveska made a wise decision. She chose Gilly.'

100

It was Gilly's turn to receive interested looks from the people around them.

Marcia whispered, 'You really are top of the Lynx pops!', which made her feel even more embarrassed.

But Gilly had a vital question for Sonia and Lenka. 'Why me? Why give your string bag to me and not to Fritz Rainer? Wouldn't that have been safer?'

'No,' said Sonia. 'For us from Bucania, it would have been unwise. With respect to Fritz, if any news of the Pendant arriving in Heldenstadt at the same time as us had leaked out, it would have been proof to Zoulok and Srot – proof that we had taken the Pendant out of Grodnik. Then things might have been very, very difficult for us when we returned to Bucania.'

There was silence while everyone thought about Sonia's remarks. Fritz nodded his head as if to say, 'she's right!'

Then Sonia turned to Lenka. 'Okay, Zaveska. Why did you choose Gilly to look after your valuable load?'

A grin flashed across the little gymnast's face. 'She was the first friend I made in this city. I was certain that she would do a good job for us.'

Kind words, thought Gilly as everyone laughed. But she won't ever know how close I was to throwing those balls in the rubbish bin. My goodness, what a lot there is to think over.

Fritz cleared his throat. 'Please listen, my friends. We are now all going to Schloss Landskron where the Löwenherz Pendant will be returned to the city of Heldenstadt. So bring your coats and go to the coaches at the gateway!'

Before they left the Academy, Gilly asked Fritz if she could hold the Pendant for a moment.

The red jewels, set in their lionheart design, flashed at her. She thought as she looked at the Pendant, You have given me more fear than bravery. Please now give me a tiny bit of courage in return.

101

Chapter 11

So Gilly, after quickly changing into a blouse and skirt, went to Schloss Landskron for a second time. On this occasion, the old castle was floodlit and could be seen from all over Heldenstadt.

As their coach drew closer to the hill, Marcia grew more and more excited. 'Stunning!' she cried as she looked up at the towers whose stern outline was softened by the lights. But she was not so pleased when she found that they had to walk up some steep stone steps to the castle. The road below the old walls was too narrow to take the coach.

Fritz Rainer and Sonia Krasna had asked that the return of the Pendant be kept secret for the time being, certainly until the Dynamo Club had been back in Grodnik for some time.

But when the Lynx party reached the courtyard, Gilly realized that the news of the Pendant's arrival had travelled far and fast. The courtyard was full of people, including the Burgermeister of Heldenstadt. They were all dressed, as Gilly told her family later, in suits and dresses as if they were going to church.

Which they were. The castle staff directed the crowd into the castle's chapel. Gilly and Marcia were about to go in as well, when Fritz took them aside. With him were Trudi and Lenka who smiled warmly when they saw their British friends. They, too, were no longer in tracksuits but wore blouses and skirts.

'Ladies,' said Fritz, 'Maria has asked you to take part in a ceremony to mark the return of the Pendant to Heldenstadt. Yes?' He stopped and looked at each of them. Without hesitation, all four nodded.

Fritz then told them what they had to do in the chapel. To her surprise, Gilly was given a small, white satin cushion to hold. On the cushion, Fritz carefully laid the Löwenherz Pendant. Its red jewels glistened even in the dim lights of the courtyard.

Benno appeared in the chapel doorway and beckoned to them.

'All is ready,' said Fritz. 'We must go in now.'

The chapel was lit by candles and low lights. It was crowded and some people had to stand, among them the gymnasts from the Academy – Austrians, Swedes, Bucanians and British. With them were their coaches including John Hanley, Natasha Oakley, Christine Nesbitt, Sonia Krasna and Gretel Hoffmann.

The most important people in Heldenstadt were there, too. As well as the Bergermeister and Herr Reinhard Ettlin, city councillors, church leaders and men and women from many organizations in the region were present. All had come to witness an event important as any in the long history of Heldenstadt.

The Countess Maria Anastasia von Löwenherz stood proud and erect below the altar steps. She wore a white dress and her fair hair which flowed down to her shoulders was held by a slim and sparkling tiara.

To the sound of soft organ music, a small procession approached her, coming slowly down the centre aisle. Leading were Lenka Zaveska and Gilly Denham. Behind them, as an escort, came Marcia Cherry and Trudi Kessler.

Lenka and Gilly halted in front of Maria. The music stopped. Maria looks exactly like a fairy-tale princess, thought Gilly.

Lenka took the Pendant by its gold chain from the cushion which Gilly carried. Holding the chain in both hands, she lifted the Pendant above her.

In a clear voice, she said: 'In the spirit of peace, in the hope of future comradeship, and in the name of the People's Republic of Bucania, I return to you this Lionheart Pendant of Heldenstadt. From now on, may it be a vital symbol – a symbol of a lasting link between our peoples.'

The little gymnast moved forward and placed the Pendant around Maria's neck. She then reached up, flung her arms around her, and kissed her. She then stepped back to stand with Gilly again. Around them, the chapel was still as the audience watched every move and listened to every word.

Maria looked at Lenka with affection. 'On behalf of the city of Heldenstadt, I thank the People's Republic of Bucania. I thank you for restoring this much-loved Pendant to its rightful place. Now more than ever may its lionheart crest inspire the courage, dedication and sacrifice that make heroes in every age. And I pledge that I shall work towards building enduring bonds of friendship – friendship between the citizens of our two countries.'

To Gilly's embarrassment, Maria had something else to say to the people in the chapel. 'Speaking of heroes, I would like to mention these two friends – Lenka Zaveska and Gilly Denham. Both went through great danger to bring this Pendant back here. We in Heldenstadt will honour them always for their bravery and determination. Lenka, Gilly . . . our thanks are just not enough for what you did so unselfishly.'

It was Maria's turn to kiss Lenka. Then she turned to Gilly and kissed her, too. Gilly struggled to stop tears coming to her eyes as Maria embraced her. It's crazy, she told herself. I didn't do anything brave.

Next, Maria lifted the gold chain of the Pendant over her head. Holding the Pendant high in front of her, she showed it to the audience, first to one side of the chapel and then to the other. Then, she raised the glittering piece of jewellery to the painting of Countess Hemma, as if to make sure that her famous ancestor knew that the Pendant had been returned to Schloss Landskron.

Finally, Maria took the Pendant and placed it carefully on the black velvet in the glass case where it had always belonged. After 200 years, the Löwenherz Pendant had finally returned home.

* * *

The rest of the evening passed in a blur for Gilly. After the ceremony in the chapel, everyone who had come to it was asked to a reception in the castle hall. There was plenty of food and drink and, after Herr Ettlin had made a welcoming speech, Gilly found she had a wonderful opportunity to get to know Lenka and the Bucanians better.

She also had to tell her adventures again to a rapt audience, including members of Lynx. Even Caroline Mayhew forgot her jealousy of Gilly in her interest to find out what exactly had happened to her. Everyone was thrilled to hear of her chase, capture and escape, and many local people thanked her repeatedly for saving the Pendant.

In the end, Gilly managed to slip away with Marcia, Trudi and Lenka to the sitting room where they had had tea on their last visit.

'It's out of this world,' said Marcia, looking out at the view of the lights of Heldenstadt below them and munching a piece of Obstkuchen, or fruit shortcake.

Suddenly, Gilly felt very tired. She had, after all, had a long, strenuous day – a day full of exercise, excitement and drama. She began to yawn, trying not to fall asleep in a very comfortable armchair.

Maria bustled in, still in her white dress. She took one look at Gilly and dashed off to find Christine.

'Benno will take her to the Academy,' she told the Lynx coach. 'She must be so exhausted.'

'She's been marvellous,' said Christine. 'You'd never think that she's done so much today. Yes, you're right. She must go to bed. We've got our final display first thing in the morning and we don't want Gilly too pooped out.'

'Come on, Gills,' urged Marcia. 'Time to go shuteye. I'm coming with you.'

Gilly hardly knew how she got back to the Academy

and her snug bed, but she had one of the best sleeps she had ever had. Next morning, she woke refreshed and full of energy. With a jolt, she realized that it was their last full day in Heldenstadt. Tomorrow, Lynx were flying back to Britain.

But first, the club had to perform its last display. Soon after that, they would hear whether they had been selected for the grand finale in the Heldenhalle. Whatever happened, Gilly needed to finish her shopping for presents for her family and new friends. Time was quickly running out.

'Let's make this display our best!' cried John as he shooed the Lynx girls into their coach after breakfast. He was anxious that the group's routine should keep to a high standard so the club could leave Heldenstadt with the reputation of being one of the best clubs in the whole *gymnaestrada*.

All the Lynx coaches were delighted at how the display had turned out. Natasha Oakley was especially pleased that a mixed crowd of gymnasts had been transformed into a skilful group of dancers. 'All of you have put so much effort into making the routine a success,' she told the girls before they arrived at the converted ice rink. And I would like to thank you all for making our time together a great pleasure for me.'

To the club's surprise, the old ice rink was packed with spectators.

"I'm sure they haven't come to see us,' said Marcia as she began to warm up, 'Look, the Bucanians are here, too. And I bet news of the Pendant is spreading far and wide. So lots of folks will want to have a look at the Grodnik girls before they go home.'

Whatever the reason for the large crowd, the applause for the Bucanians was long and loud, both before and after their display.

'They've got a wonderful routine,' said Gilly in admiration. 'It's worth coming all this way just to see it alone.'

But the Lynx girls also received generous praise. They were now able to enjoy themselves to the full without feeling nervous. Smiles from their coaches told them that their performance, too, had been a good one. And Trudi and Maria were elated that the club which they had been looking after had produced another successful routine.

'Shame we aren't doing any more displays,' observed Shani Patel dreamily in the coach on the way back to the Academy.

'Well, you never know,' said Gilly. 'With a bit of luck we could . . . this evening.'

Christine said, 'Fritz will be able to tell us at lunchtime which clubs will be in the finale. So everyone must be back in the Academy by then to find out whether we are needed at the Heldenhalle. In any case, there's a sightseeing trip arranged for this afternoon.'

After they had changed, Gilly and Marcia went out to finish their shopping. Maria and Trudi could not come with them as they were wanted by the Löwenherz club for practice. Löwenherz were appearing in the finale in any case because they were a host club.

By the time Gilly got back to the Academy, she had been able to buy all the presents she needed. For her mother, there was a bright red scarf. For her father, she had bought a drawing of St Michael's Cathedral. And for Richard, she had a little carved figure of an Austrian man in traditional costume – breeches, waistcoat and hat with a sprig of blossom.

She had not forgotten her Austrian friends, either. Maria's present was a little picture frame. And for Trudi she had found a small, decorated bowl. Finally, she had decided to get Lenka a little wooden box with simple carved decorations on the lid.

After lunch, there was no sign of Fritz Rainer. The Lynx girls began to get bored and restless with waiting, not wanting to waste their last afternoon.

Finally, John said, trying to keep the disappointment out of his voice. 'It looks as if we haven't been chosen for the finale. Right, all aboard for some sight-seeing!'

But just as their coach was about to pull away, Fritz drove up in a taxi, his face beaming. '*Sehr gut!* Very good!' he called out. 'Lynx are invited to take part this evening! Congratulations!'

There were shouts and gasps of delight all over the coach. Everyone knew exactly what they had achieved. They were going to end their week at the *gymnaestrada* in company with some of the best gymnastics groups in the world. And they, Lynx, had shown what British gymnasts could do.

For the next few hours, the coach whirled the girls around Heldenstadt old and new. Among the places they visited were the ancient county hall, the botanical gardens and the city zoo. They also went into the cathedral of St Michael, and the city museum and art gallery.

'It's a great place,' said Marcia, 'but give me Lincston any day. It's too exciting here!'

During their trip, Gilly had noticed something. 'Look,' she pointed out to her friend. 'A lot of the buildings are flying Löwenherz flags.'

'Well,' said Marcia, 'just as I thought. No one could keep the return of the Pendant a secret, could they? Even if nothing's been said about it. Heavens, I should think this evening's going to be pretty exciting!'

To Gilly, their final evening in the Heldenhalle, the hall of the heroes, was more than exciting. It was sensationally thrilling.

The Heldenhalle was a square-shaped building, with row upon row of seats on three sides going up from the arena to the roof. From what Gilly could see, as she waited with the Lynx team to march on, every one of the thousands of seats was filled.

The finale was the climax of the *gymnaestrada*. The best clubs and groups in the festival would perform in a feast of gymnastic talent. They would first march on for the opening ceremony by the Bergermeister and then perform their routines in turn.

But there was a rousing atmosphere in the hall – an atmosphere caused not just by the coming gymnastics displays and the carnival spirit of the big brass band playing there. There was also a feeling of expectation in the vast crowd as if a very special event was about to take place.

There was no doubt now that most of the citizens of Heldenstadt had heard of the return of the Löwenherz Pendant. And many, too, had learned something of how it had come back to the city.

When the Lynx girls arrived at the hall entrance, they were greeted with a burst of applause by a small bunch of onlookers.

'That's for you,' chuckled Marcia to Gilly. 'You're famous around here.'

Ahead of them, clubs were marching in to the arena after being announced to the spectators. The United States, Japan, West Germany, Denmark – wherever they came from, all the groups were warmly greeted. Then it was the turn of Lynx.

'Lynx, Lincston!' boomed the loudspeakers.

As the yellow leotards of Lynx swept into the arena the burst of clapping and cheering from the huge crowd was the loudest yet. Almost bewildered by their reception, the girls took their place in the line-up beside the Danish team.

The welcome given to the following teams from Finland

110

and Hong Kong did not match that of Lynx but the next one more than did.

'Dynamo, Grodnik!' cried the announcer.

At the opening ceremony, the Bucanian girls had almost slunk into the stadium, accompanied by booing and jeering. But this time, they entered with pride, holding their heads high, and waving happily. The audience responded with tumultous enthusiasm, many jumping to their feet to clap and wave back, all hailing the blue leotards as honoured guests.

At last! thought Gilly. No more anger. No more insults. Bucania, too, has truly come back to Heldenstadt.

But the next entry – the last one – brought the most thunderous applause of all.

'Löwenherz, Heldenstadt!'

Every single person in the Heldenhalle jumped to his or her feet. Cheering, shouting, clapping, stamping, everyone, including the visiting teams, acclaimed the city's own renowned club. The arena echoed with roars of 'Löwenherz! Löwenherz!'

'Yes!' called Marcia over the noise. 'They know about the Pendant!'

As the parade of light green leotards swung into view, the excitement grew to deafening heights. There, leading the gymnasts in and looking regal even in her leotard, was Maria Löwenherz. However, it was what she carried that made the vast crowd burst out with even more emotion.

It was a large white, heart-shaped banner on which was a red lion placed sideways and showing its claws.

As the plane taking the Lincston Gymnastics Club back to Britain the next day flew over the Alps, Gilly sat silent in her seat, mulling over the memories of the last week. Some were fun, others scary. But all were exciting. To think that she had nearly missed the trip altogether!

111

Last night, there had been a smashing party at the Academy ending with a firework display. The Lynx boys had come along, too. At the party, John had presented Fritz, Gretel, Maria and Trudi with Lynx club shields and flowers to thank them for looking after the club during the *gymnaestrada*. He also asked them to visit Lincston before long.

Gilly, too, handed her presents to Maria, Trudi and Lenka.

To her delight, Lenka gave her a tiny set of wooden Russian dolls which all fitted inside each other. The little gymnast said, her eyes moist, 'I will keep all my secrets in your box. For ever.'

As they said goodbye that morning, Lenka declared, 'We will meet somewhere again, Gilly Denham. By then, I know you will be a champion!'

Gilly's biggest surprise was that Trudi had organized a collection among the girls of the Löwenherz club. They had then bought for Gilly 'Victoria', the doll which she had admired and which she had mentioned when she told her friends about her chase in the flea market.

But she was proudest of all of a present given to her by Maria and Trudi – their club badge. 'You are now a member of Löwenherz, Heldenstadt,' said Maria. 'You must come and stay with us whenever you can.' Maria also gave her a little silver Löwenherz brooch in thanks.

Dozily, Gilly became aware that Christine was standing in the aisle and talking to her. 'I want you down at the gym first thing after school tomorrow. In case you've forgotten, we're going to Wembley next weekend. And that means we've got to catch up on some vital training.'

Gilly caught Marcia's eye and they burst into giggles. Marcia winked as if to say, 'You're back in business!'

Chapter 12

GYMNAST GILLY
– LYNX SUPERGIRL

When Gilly ran out of the passage at Wembley Arena, the brightness of the lights made her blink. Trying not to stumble, she climbed the wooden steps to the podium ahead of the boy competitor she was paired with.

The arena announcer at the competition control desk

called out through his microphone: 'From the south zone, Gilly Denham and Robert Morehouse!'

There was a burst of applause from the surrounding stands as Gilly ran across the 12-metre floor mat, waving to the spectators with a timid smile. A television camera turned to follow her into the line-up of the other competitors.

The yellow Lynx banner with its message *Gymnast Gilly – Lynx Supergirl* caught her eye. She gave her friends a special wave to thank them for their support. Up there in the crowded stand, too, were her parents who had backed her so wonderfully. Now she must show everybody that she deserved their loyalty.

Come on, Gilly, she said to herself again. Don't be such a funk. You've been through more frightening times than this. Like in Heldenstadt. Remember?

The television commentator was telling her vast unseen audience, 'In the yellow tracksuit, we have Gilly Denham from the Lincston Gymnastics Club. Gilly only just qualified for these grand finals in this her first big national competition. We will have to see whether she has the experience to get near a medal position, considering she has got to face some tough opposition.'

The toughest opposition for most of the gymnasts there was, of course, Mary Weston, the tall gymnast from Yorkshire whom Christine had warned Gilly about before. Mary, a serious-looking girl in a navy blue leotard with white stripes, was considered the best gymnast in the competition by many experts. She was thus the most likely winner.

But there was another outstanding gymnast with an excellent chance of becoming the champion that afternoon. She was Samantha Padmore, a friendly Afro-Caribbean girl from Manchester who was wearing a bright

114

scarlet leotard. Samantha was a member of one of the junior national squads.

When the 16 gymnasts were all standing in one long line facing the main stand, the military band played the national anthem. Then the band broke into a march and the competitors strode off to warm up for the first round of the event.

For the girls, the first piece was, as usual, the vault. While she waited for her turn, Gilly sat still with Christine at the west end of the arena and tried to quell her nervousness. She knew she must put rivals such as Mary and Samantha from her mind and concentrate on the job ahead of her.

Christine wisely did not say anything to her. All she had to say had been said during the week of hard training which they had tackled after their return from Austria. Now, wearing a yellow Lynx tracksuit, she would stay close to Gilly throughout the competition.

Once the competition had started, Gilly began to feel much more at ease. Although she had warmed up thoroughly before the crowd had taken their seats, she decided to continue with some further limbering up.

Under the stands, many of the young spectators were bustling about the concourse, buying hamburgers and drinks at the last moment to eat as they watched the action in the arena.

In the east stand, Marcia was set to keep score. In order not to influence the judging, the placings of the gymnasts were not revealed until the end of the event. So to keep track of how Gilly was doing, Marcia wrote down the points scored by each gymnast with the aim of adding them up as the competition proceeded.

Fingers crossed, thought Marcia as the first boy came on to the podium for his floor exercise and the first girl prepared to spring over the vaulting horse at the end of the running mat. As usual, each girl was permitted two vaults, with her official score being the higher of the two. With her first attempt, Mary Weston hit 9.30 with a handspring piked front somersault. Her supporters jumped up and down with glee.

'Phew!' said Marcia to Melanie Wood who was sitting beside her. 'That could be a winner.' She wrote down '9.30' on her scoresheet.

Reluctantly, Melanie agreed. Mary's vault was, in fact, excellent and set a very high standard for the competition.

Soon after, Samantha Padmore came up with 9.20 for her handspring full twist. A big grin lit up her face. She and Mary were now in the lead.

Gilly's first attempt at her piked Tsukahara was disastrous. She under-rotated coming off the vaulting horse and fell forward on to her hands when she landed.

In the stand, Marcia moaned. '8.80!' She knew her friend could do better. Around her, the Lynx girls sat silent with anxiety.

Christine, who was standing near the vaulting horse, tried not to show her disappointment. 'Relax, Gilly,' she said as they walked back to the beginning of the running strip. 'You've got the speed; now try and get more height. As you've always done.'

With a worried frown, Gilly nodded. She realized that her second vault had to be a big improvement. Otherwise, she had no chance of catching the leaders, let alone being near them.

The green light on the electronic scoreboard flashed on. Gilly presented herself to the head judge and then switched her attention to the vaulting horse 20 metres ahead of her. This is it, Gilly, she told herself. If you don't get it now, you never will.

She leaned forward and sped down the mat.

Marcia did not dare to look. She shut her eyes, only to open them quickly when clapping and delighted cries broke out from the Lynx party surrounding her. Their banner waved jubilantly.

There was Gilly, pleased as pleased, presenting herself to the head judge again. This time, her piked Tsukahara had been smashing. There was no doubt about that. And her landing had been rock-solid.

The television announcer agreed. 'That second vault by Gilly Denham is a big improvement,' she confided to millions of viewers. 'It will certainly startle some of her better-known competitors.'

The scoreboard lit up with '9.10' which a joyful Marcia wrote on her scoresheet. That wasn't a bad start. But there was still a huge gap between Gilly and the leaders. Deep in her heart, Marcia felt that her friend must now be out of the running.

The next apparatus was the asymmetric bars. Mary Weston had no difficulty keeping her lead by scoring 9.00. But Samantha Padmore's routine lost its smooth rhythm and there were several noticeable pauses in it. The judges gave Samantha 8.75.

At the far end of the arena, Robert Morehouse completed his rings exercise, revolving off the apparatus with a back somersault.

Immediately afterwards, Gilly went on to the bars. She wore handguards to protect her palms and her hands were covered with 'chalk', the magnesium carbonate powder which would help to reduce friction and make her grasp on the bars slippery. Christine gave her a pat on the shoulder and squatted close to the apparatus to keep a careful eye on her.

In the stand, Marcia held her breath, holding her pencil up to her mouth. The entire Lynx party were silent in the suspense of hoping that Gilly would produce a really cracking routine – a routine which could bring her closer to the leaders.

Marcia knew Gilly's asymmetric bars routine as well as Gilly herself. 'Good girl,' she said under her breath. 'You're doing all right.'

A nearby television camera held Gilly in its picture and several press photographers were clicking away as she swept through her routine, her confidence growing.

She finished the exercise with a near-perfect giant swing and an expert front somersault off, but she took an extra step on landing.

Drat! thought Gilly. The judges could hardly miss that. But she smiled, and presented herself to the head judge again.

Marcia's eyes swivelled to the bars scoreboard. Within a few seconds, Gilly's score flashed up: 9.00 dead – same as Mary Weston! Now that was encouraging. Keep it up, Gills, she called out silently. It would be fabulous, just wonderful if you just got into the first three.

Once again, Gilly had a rest before she went on the beam. Once again, she could watch her Northern rivals – Mary and Samantha – perform ahead of her. Out of the corner of her eye, she was aware that the boys were completing their rings exercises and starting to vault.

Several Lynx girls took the opportunity to run down to the concourse to buy crisps and sausage rolls.

Marcia sat gloomily watching Mary Weston at work on the 10-centimetre wide, chamois leather-covered strip of wood. The arena was totally still. The Yorkshire girl had a tip-top routine, that was for sure.

Oh, no!

The gasp from the crowd rippled around the arena. Mary had wobbled, overbalanced, and had fallen from the beam.

Bad luck on Mary, thought Marcia, but that .50 penalty is certainly going to help Gilly. Her spirits began to rise again.

Mary remounted the beam again within the required time of 30 seconds and carried on with her routine. But the fall had clearly shaken her determination, and she tottered dangerously again when she went from a split leap to a half turn.

Mary dismounted with a superb front somersault with full twist but the damage was done. The judges could not give her more than 8.60. Marcia gave a great sigh of relief as she marked the score down.

After Samantha had also fallen from the beam during her beam and had scored 8.30, Gilly and Christine looked at each other with their eyebrows raised. While they did not know Gilly's position in the competition at that time, they both sensed that the two falls had given Gilly a fresh chance of catching up.

Provided, of course, she stayed on the beam herself.

Christine said in a quiet voice, 'You just show them!'

Just before Gilly's turn on the beam, both she and Christine realized that she had become the centre of a great deal of interest.

Most of the photographers were now clustered a few metres away, their cameras at the ready and all aimed at her. Three television cameramen were poised to capture her routine for the outside world, and arena stewards were trying to prevent spectators from filling the neighbouring entrance doorways to get a closer look at her.

Near the beam, the green light on the scoreboard signalled the go-ahead. Gilly paused for a few seconds, forcing herself to think of nothing else but her familiar routine which had taken her through the other stages of the Junior Champion Gymnast competition. She tried not to remember that she had a very weak point in her exercise. This was her aerial cartwheel, a cartwheel without using the arms.

She began her routine, watched in complete silence by the big crowd. The routine contained its usual features: cartwheel mount, split leap to split leap, back flip to back flip, back walkover . . .

So far, so good. But Marcia was sweating as Gilly started her dreaded aerial. You've just got to, she again appealed in silence to her friend, you've just got to stay on!

Gilly's feet came down with a thud on to the beam. Her landing was so secure that she showed hardly a trace of a waver as she regained her balance. Marcia, Christine and all the Lynx supporters practically sobbed in relief.

Round off, double twisting somersault dismount . . . at last Gilly's routine was over. Another safe landing earned her a burst of enthusiastic clapping.

Marcia waved and waved as if Gilly could see her in the depth of the crowd. 'Well done! Well done!' she cried. Then she picked up her scoresheet and began to add the figures up. Samantha Padmore had 26.25 and Mary Weston was still in the lead with 26.90. She waited impatiently for Gilly's beam score.

But the score was delayed. The judges at the beam got together for a conference with the head judge to discuss the marking of Gilly's exercise.

'Come on!' snorted Marcia impatiently. 'Why keep everyone waiting?'

After what seemed ages, the judges returned to their seats and at last the score was flashed up . . . 8.80.

Not bad again, thought Marcia as she casually added up Gilly's score – and sat back unbelieving. 26.90? That was the same as Mary Weston's. Marcia checked again. Goodness! She was right. Gilly had caught up. Gilly was now sharing the lead!

With a shriek of astonishment, Marcia waved her scoresheet at her friends. 'Gilly's tied with Mary! She can win it! She can win it!'

The Lynx girls clapped their hands and squealed with glee and waved their banner energetically.

And then the banner stopped waving as the girls realized whom Gilly had to beat to win. As Christine had said, Mary Weston was one of the best floor performers of her age in the whole of Britain.

We need a miracle, thought Marcia, her delight turning to depression.

The television commentator explained the situation to the viewers. She, too, was caught up in the excitement which was now sweeping through the arena. 'Here we have a big surprise. Gilly Denham has drawn level in first place with Mary Weston! Gilly Denham of Lincston, who was not expected to make anything like such a strong challenge.'

One of the television cameras swung around to put Gilly on screen again as she began more limbering up.

The TV commentator continued: 'And what a fight we're going to see! The winner, the Junior Champion Girl Gymnast, must now be decided by the last piece . . . the floor exercise!'

The girls' floor routines began at the same time as the spectacular horizontal bar exercises of the boys. To many of the spectators, these two final events were the most dramatic part of the afternoon. To add to the tension felt by her friends, Gilly was the last performer of the whole competition.

At first, Marcia could not bear to stay in her seat. She got up and went below to the concourse where she paced up and down, unable to watch Gilly's ordeal.

Gilly had no idea, of course, that she shared the lead with Mary Weston. She continued to limber up quietly, every now and then watching the boys circle the horizontal bar. She did not want to look at the other floor routines but her ears could not block out the taped music to which her rivals were performing.

Her own music for her one minute twenty second routine was a medley of tunes taken from a famous old opera, *Carmen* by Bizet. She knew every note of her tape and what she had to do over the entire area of the 12-metre floor mat.

There was a hush as Mary Weston came on to the floor. When she began, the audience watched every step, every gesture she made. Like all floor exercises, Mary's routine included dance movements, acrobatics, turns, jumps and balances.

When Mary had finished her last tumble run with an expert full twisting back somersault, the same move which Gilly was using, the crowd applauded loudly. It certainly was a hard performance for Gilly to beat.

But Christine sensed that Mary's movements did not quite match her music effectively. The judges delayed the score and held another conference, before awarding Mary 8.75.

In a few minutes, it was time for Gilly's floor exercise. Melanie Wood shot down to the concourse to find Marcia. 'Come on, Marce!' she yelled. 'Gilly's on . . . any moment! She's got to beat 8.75!'

Marcia ran back to her seat, hardly bearing to look, but knowing she had to watch her friend, win or lose.

Before Gilly could begin her exercise, she had to wait by the podium steps for the final horizontal bar routine to finish. For a moment, she thought of the lionheart crest of Heldenstadt and the courage it stood for. She resolved there and then to make both her clubs – Lynx and Löwenherz – proud of her in her final performance, proud no matter what her finishing position was.

Then the competition steward touched her arm and nodded. The arena announcer called, 'The last competitor of the Junior Champion Gymnast competition . ... Gilly Denham!'

This was it. Now or never. Do or die. Up she went on to the floor mat. For the last time she presented herself to the head judge. Then she crouched down in the centre of the mat, waiting for her music to start.

The whole crowd, Lynx girls included, sat in silence, gripped by the last act of the drama, all watching the lonely, yellow leotard.

Marcia said afterwards, 'Your style and dance movements were super. I bet our week in Heldenstadt did you a power of good. But your gymnastic moves! I knew you could slip up on them anytime.'

But once her music had begun, Gilly concentrated on nothing but the order and quality of the moves she had to carry out. From the opening notes, she made the moves more than a basic demonstration of skills. Tucked front somersault, walkout, round off, back flip, whatever she tackled . . . it became part of a continuous flowing sequence.

Then her music changed rhythm as it launched into the catchy tune of Bizet's Habeñera. The huge audience began to clap in time to the beat as she put her whole being into the piece, gymnast and dancer all in one.

Finally, Gilly landed her full twisting back somersault fairly and squarely. She completed her routine by shrinking to her starting position . . . a crouch in the middle of the mat. On the last chord of the music, she sat back quickly and thrust her arms towards the roof.

The whole arena exploded into clapping and cheering. Marcia sat with tears streaming down her face.

In a daze, Gilly left the podium. Christine hugged her and took her off to put on her yellow tracksuit. 'You couldn't have done better,' she said proudly. 'Now hurry up. You've got to march in for the medal presentation ceremony.'

The band struck up and the gymnasts marched in two by two through the big doors at the end of the arena up on to the podium. They lined up as they had at the beginning of the competition. Now they would know the results. In front of them were placed the rostrums marked 1, 2 and 3, the little platforms where the medal winners would stand.

The party of top officials and sponsors who were to present the awards came on to the podium. With them were the young competition runners who carried the medals and trophies on red trays.

The arena announcer gave out the results announcing the third-placed winners first. 'Samantha Padmore!' he boomed to the audience. Waving as cheerfully as she could, Samantha jumped on to the rostrum with Robert Morehouse who had also won a bronze medal.

'In second place,' cried the announcer, 'with a score of 35.65 . . . Mary Weston!' For a second, the Yorkshire girl's face fell with disappointment. Then she, too, ran out of the line-up with a smile on to the silver medal rostrum.

Gosh, thought Gilly, if Mary hasn't pulled it off, I wonder who has?

The generous applause for her rival died away. Who *had* won in such a close finish? The spectators sat still, agog for the final result.

The announcer took a deep breath. 'And the winner, the new Junior Champion Girl Gymnast of all Britain, with a score of 35.70 . . . Gilly Denham!'

There was a brief pause. Then wave upon wave of clapping and cheering filled the entire building. The Lynx girls were screaming in triumph, their banner waving like a battle flag. 'Gymnast Gilly – Lynx Supergirl!' they cried again and again. Marcia ran to Mr and Mrs Denham and the three of them hugged each other, unable to speak.

Gilly stood, helpless with amazement, hardly believing what she had heard. She couldn't have beaten Mary Weston. Never. She couldn't have.

Then the girl beside her gave her a push. 'Go on! You've won!'

Gilly staggered forward. How she mounted the winner's rostrum, she had no idea. She found herself standing beside the boy winner, holding the immense champion's trophy, and waving to the four sides of the arena. I don't deserve this, she thought, but thank you, thank you all my friends, all my family, for your help . . .

Afterwards, Gilly took away many memories of that afternoon. Such as posing for photographs on the podium holding her huge trophy; being congratulated by the top people in British gymnastics; greeting Marcia, Christine, her family and all her friends who were so proud of her; and being interviewed on television.

The television interview was held on a balcony over-looking the podium on which she had achieved her narrow victory.

Gilly sat shyly in her yellow tracksuit, waiting for the television crew to set their camera and lights in position.

'Fantastic, Gilly,' said the famous personality who was going to interview her, herself a former British gymnastics champion. 'You really have got a wonderful future ahead of you. By the way, I know your own Lynx club badge, but what's the other one – with the lion? What does that stand for?'

'Well,' said Gymnast Gilly, touching the heart-shaped badge with her fingers. 'I suppose it stands for never giving up . . . whatever you're doing, wherever you are.'

STEVIE DAY SUPERSLEUTH
(that's me!)

I'm on my way to being the first female Commis-
sioner of the Metropolitan Police. It's true I have a
few personal problems: for a start I'm small and
skinny and people are always mistaking me for a
boy. I'm 14 – though you wouldn't think so – and
my younger sister, Carla, not only looks older than
me but she's much prettier too. Not that that really
matters. You see, she doesn't have my brains.

If you want to see my razor-sharp mind in action or
have proof of my brilliant powers of deduction then
read about my triumphant successes in:

STEVIE DAY: Supersleuth
STEVIE DAY: Lonely Hearts
STEVIE DAY: Rat Race

Have you seen
NANCY DREW
lately?

Nancy Drew has become a girl of the 80s! There is hardly a girl from seven to seventeen who doesn't know her name.

Now you can continue to enjoy Nancy Drew in a new series, written for older readers – THE NANCY DREW FILES. Each book has more romance, fashion, mystery and adventure.

In THE NANCY DREW FILES, Nancy pursues one thrilling adventure after another. With her boundless energy and intelligence, Nancy finds herself enrolling at a crime-ridden high school, attending rock concerts and locating the missing star, skiing in Vermont with friends Bess and George and faithful boyfriend Ned, and temping at a teenage magazine based in wildly exciting New York.

COMING IN SPRING 1988

The Nancy Drew Files

No. 1 Secrets Can Kill
No. 2 Deadly Intent
No. 3 Murder on Ice
No. 4 Smile and Say Murder

ARMADA

'JINNY' BOOKS
by Patricia Leitch

When Jinny Manders rescues Shantih, a chestnut Arab, from a cruel circus, her dreams of owning a horse of her own seem to come true. But Shantih is wild and unrideable.

This is an exciting and moving series of books about a very special relationship between a girl and a magnificent horse.

FOR LOVE OF A HORSE
A DEVIL TO RIDE
THE SUMMER RIDERS
NIGHT OF THE RED HORSE
GALLOP TO THE HILLS
HORSE IN A MILLION
THE MAGIC PONY
RIDE LIKE THE WIND
CHESTNUT GOLD
JUMP FOR THE MOON
HORSE OF FIRE

Armada